## FROM THE DOCUMENTARY,
### *Orbital Art Blues*
### BY CY YEAWORTH:

[Pablo gently hits one of Firedrop's sculptures. It starts vibrating on the rods it's suspended from.]

CORTEZ: Beautiful. They have no up or down—reminds us that the gravity here is inmitación. Este es la nueva environment realisida. This is what space art should be.

[Firedrop steps closer to him; the floating parts of her dress press against him, obscuring his hands.]

FIREDROP: Yes! Yes! You get it, you understand what I'm trying to do! Is your art freefall-oriented?

[They move closer until their bodies touch.]

CORTEZ: I want it to be. Muy mucho. I proposed a freefall abstract-expressionist painting project to the Space Culture Project board for this Festival, but it was el rejecto grande.

[Firedrop pouts.]

FIREDROP: I know how that is. I wanted my pieces to be displayed in freefall—you know, like suspended in electromagnetic fields or something like that, but they said it wasn't feasible.

[They run their hands over each other's bodies.]

CORTEZ: Ay, chiquita! I know, they just don't know when to leave an artist alone.

[Their faces move together. They kiss.]

FIREDROP: I definitely see what you mean.

[They kiss again. She leans into him. They drop to the ground. Finally an article of clothing is thrown at the camera . . .]

# From Tor Books

BEN BOVA'S DISCOVERIES

BEN BOVA PRESENTS

*forthcoming

# BEN BOVA'S Discoveries

# Cortez On Jupiter

## Ernest Hogan

A TOM DOHERTY ASSOCIATES BOOK
NEW YORK

CORTEZ ON JUPITER

Copyright © 1990 by Ernest Hogan

A Tor Book
Published by Tom Doherty Associates, Inc.
49 West 24th Street
New York, N.Y. 10010

Cover art by Ron Walotsky

ISBN: 0-812-50236-1

First edition: June 1990

Printed in the United States of America

0 9 8 7 6 5 4 3 2 1

New art is sensory violence
           on the frontiers of experience.

—Marshall McLuhan, *Culture Is Our Business*

# = 1 =

## Intro

Yeah, yeah, I know that that big chingada System-famous II superstar reporter Ms. Anna Paik is due here a little while ago, but—ay, ay, ay, that blob of paint! It just hangs there in the very center of my splatterpaint studio like a miniature Jupiter gone todo loco—the big planet with tides and weather and gravitísimo snapped on the strain of the mindscrambling secret of its monstrous microscopic inhabitants so's its regular bands get all broken up into merrily swirling asymmetrical patterns of mingling paint of cyberexaggerated color—like the glorious, unholy mama of all cat's-eye marbles, it glares at me.

I try not to see that Zulu bitch.

I'm so glad there's no gravity here, no está aquí, no way, nada . . . but that floating glob had a pull just the same. I orbit in freefall, make the cabrones let me paint here in the center of Ithaca Base where the spinning doesn't suck you to the floor like the irresistible pull of Jupiter—so big, so bad, so goddamn awesome that as you fall into those convulsive, frenzied clouds, you feel like you're being sucked *up*, not pulled down—Jupiter is too big, too gigantic for you ever to be on top of it—and it's *still* pulling me.

And she still pulls me.

"I'm gonna make you a Pablo Cortez!" I growl, and attack.

Paint stick in hand like an Aztec priest wielding a flint knife, or that cop swinging his baton on that cool starless night years ago in L.A. that crushed the buckle from my gas mask into my skull, leaving a cute scarito in my scalp that I wore my hair extra short for months to show off. Or like in that time before time when space wasn't separate from time or anything was separate from anything else and all was the goddess Coatlicue, She of the Serpent Skirt, but then she was the Cipactli monster: alligatoroid, fishoid, but more a great, quivering mass swimming in an endless sea that was also a sky, a mass with mucho, mucho hungry mouths that devoured everything, the monster, the sea, the monster, the sea, so the sea was the monster and vice versa— everything all mixed up like Siren zapware feedback—ay! Makes me want to be like the gods Quetzalcoatl and Tezcatlipoca—I wonder which I am, culture-giver or trickster? Could I be both? Why not? I know how they felt when they decided, Hey, enough of this formless nadaness! Let's tear this monster/paint blob apart!

It explodes—like an amphetamine-choked blob, like the Cipactli monster, brutally torn in half by her moving mijos, screaming as her lower half rises to become the heavens and her upper half falls to become the earth—forming the universe—but she manages to bite off Tezcatlipoca's foot in the process, so he tears off her lower jaw. Mutilated and screaming, space and time are set in motion as we move from Ometecuhtli's timelessness to Xiuhtecuhtli's fiery spinning clockwork around the North Star. What the Mayans call the Burden of Time is picked up, latches on. Amorphous micromonsters sail through the air, some colliding with me, sticking to my naked flesh and my chones. One seeks my eyes in order to blind me. Lucky I wear goggles like Tlaloc, the storm god, and a respirator—the paint just bounces off the Nostic-coated lenses.

This whole canvas-lined chamber explodes with color. Beautiful. Like her, Willa, the Zulu goddess that pollutes my Aztec pantheon.

Still, the polycrylic paint has this sickening tendency to settle into little giggling globes that just sit there like mini-Jupiters, mocking me. I refuse to allow entropy to happen in my presence, so like a samurai Jackson Pollock, I scream and thrash the disgusting buggeritos into tinier flying sky-serpents that gaily decorate the canvas on the walls.

The canvas is raw, unprimed, and the polycrylic is mixed with a base that gives it the consistency of water. Splatter marks don't just sit there looking pretty—they grow fur as the canvas absorbs it, thirstily. My work is always wild and woolly.

Soon the colorful swordplay is over and I am victorious. All the paint (except for a few stubborn, but insignificant BBs) is slapped into the canvas. I shed my goggles awhile and the furious splatters change into visions.

André Masson, eat your heart out!

Bizarre animated hieroglyphics materialize in the Jovian storm clouds: *demonic cartoon characters exhaling balloons full of obscenity—endless 3-D labyrinths of orbital castles complete with living gargoyles and tapestries you can walk into—large, luxuriant cars encrusted in jewels and tailfins that race the crowded, tangled spaghetti of freeways with offramps all over the galaxy—the vegetal love poetry that an intelligent network of vines sings to the jungle it intricately embraces—the ecstatic rush of falling into an ocean of warm mud that tastes delicious and makes you feel so good—pornographic geometries that can only be imagined on a scale more than intergalactic—the byzantine plots of surrealistic soap operas that take place outside of spacetime in Omeyocan, the highest heaven, domain of Ometecuhtli, the Dual Lord, supreme being outside of space and time; Sirenesque, because they never picked up the burden of time either, like before I hit the paint blob or the Cipactli monster got torn apart; see my problema?—the ballet of subatomic particles smaller than any yet discovered!—et cetera et cetera et cetera. . . .*

Letting the stick fly, I attack the canvas with paint-covered fingers—desperately trying to record the visions before they fade, but never finishing before they do, so I have to fill the many gaps with memory and imagination.

I shift from warrior to artist; un poquito more Toltec than Aztec. Like that Nahuatl poem:

> *He knows colors, applies and shadows*
> *   them.*
> *Draws the feet, the faces,*
> *Sketches the shadows, obtains a finish,*

*As if he were a Toltec artist*
*He paints the total colors of flowers.*

Yeah, that's me-ish. My folks would be proud. I remember the poetry, the flowers and songs. It's important because the enemy destroyed so much of la cultura. Sí, Papa. Sí, Mama. I remember.

Then I see her face again. Willa's face— that dazzling, living African sculpture that exists somewhere between the inside of my overloaded cabeza, the zapware fireworks of the Sirens, and the frontiers of the universe. It all starts turning into her after a while . . . then tears start growing in my eyes, get bigger and bigger, and finally break away and orbit my eyes like Earthish waterplanets.

The door seal pops. It's Anna Paik, come to interview me in my unnatural habitat.

I slip the goggles over my teary eyes, let myself drift so I face the door—I've lost track of where it is (again) but: canvas starts to pucker, bulge like a zombie's grave, tearing loose from the gluespots, a large section breaks free, wraps around whoever it is that's trying to enter, then gets tossed where it hovers like a multicolor mutant jellyfish.

Then she enters. Anna Paik, the muchacha that the System loves to look at and listen to.

I can feel Willa getting jealous (they tell me it's my imagination).

Anna is awkward getting in. Even though she's been on an epic tour of the System, in and out of gravity wells for the last few years, she's still terminally grav-legged— even doing yoga facial exercises to fight facebloat, those lips, sticked the same shade of electric blond as her hair, stretch wide, clinching the light in a way that could cook my chorizo. She sees me seeing her and that cute overly-made-up-for-holo (kinda making her look like a pornette) Eurasian face popped into an instant professional smile with a flash blush and a hint of flirtation in those eyes that wore violet contacts for the occasion.

"Pablo, you started without us," she says, up close and personal, with a slight Russian accent that almost makes me forget she's wearing a bubble ziploc clear baggie suit *over* some skintight furry designer jumpsuit that's the same color as her contacts.

"I couldn't resist that paint. Hey, don't I rate those famous dark, mysterious eyes?"

Giggle giggle. "The contacts are part of the outfit, goes with the flocked toe and fingernails. We're contracted to sell it as a package. The demogs figure this'll go over big with the arty types."

"With or without the baggie?"

"Well, we couldn't let it get your paint all over it."

I get a toehold and prop myself upside down from her. "Hey, why not? It'd be a Pablo Cortez original. Real megabuck action there!"

She smiles again, really must have trained hard to get all her gravbound facial expressions to work in freefall. "We thought of that. Only the helmet is Nostic'd. We'll do a network time-lag-adjusted auction later."

"Interplanetary Infotainment thinks of everything . . . my agent know about it?"

"Of course, silly." Pause. She holds the smile while wondering if she should have called me silly. "You'll be getting a cut, II wouldn't dare cheat you."

"Yeah, not even them."

She reaches up and puts a plastic-wrapped hand on my shoulder. "Look, we want us all to look good here, with the whole System plugging in and all." The pat was a poquito too hard, sends me back, but I'm braced, and she goes into an unplanned backflip. "Whoa! I don't think I'll ever get the hang of this. Anyway, speaking of looking good, we do have a makeup man standing by—he specializes in correcting for freefall facebloat. . . ."

I peel off the goggles and respirator,

smear some paint on my face. "This is all the makeup I need."

"Okay . . . yeah . . . And are you sure that's what you want to wear?"

Her eyes are on my multilayer paint-spattered chones (and probably on what's inside them). "Ay! I put these on just for this interview! I usually paint in the nude. I figured II wasn't ready to show me with my huevos hanging out?"

She cocks her head to the side where she wears a bulky earcuff, listens to it buzz. "Huevos? Eggs? I don't understand."

"Don't tell me your translator isn't programmed for slang. . . ."

"Isn't Spanish Spanish?"

I laugh. "Yeah, like Russian is Russian and English is English all over the System. Words are words. I don't really care what language they're from—I just use 'em when they fit."

For a while her face goes inscrutable/Orientalish as if facebloat was setting in.

Now something else comes through the door—the camera, mounted on a serpentine waldostalk and wrapped in Nostic'd plastic like the head of a mechanical dragon sealed in a cocoon.

Anna vigorously stretches and clenches her face a few times, listens to her earcuff, and says, "They're ready to roll. You ready to begin?"

I nod. The red light on the camera clicks on. I flick my wrist and send the paint still clinging to my stick at her.

FROM THE UNEDITED HOLOTAPE OF THE "ANNA AT LARGE" INTERVIEW WITH PABLO CORTEZ FOR INTERPLANETARY INFOTAINMENT'S "SYSTEM NOW":

(Blobs of paint splatter on Anna's baggie.)

ANNA PAIK: Hi, everybody! This is Anna Paik, coming to you from a different place, a colorful place, a place where the activities of one man have become the focus of Systemwide attention in terms of both science and art. This is the studio of Pablo Cortez, in the central freefall module of Project Odysseus' Ithaca Base, orbiting just outside the magnetosphere of Jupiter.

(More paint splatters on Anna.)

As you can see, I'm not alone. Systemfolx, please allow me to introduce you to Pablo Cortez. . . .

(Camera quick-pans to a tight shot of Pablo, who is upside down and at a forty-five-degree angle to audience's viewpoint. He floats in semifetal posture, has the thin legs and thick, bloated chest of a spacer, and wears only undershorts and a respirator and goggles that are floating around his neck. He has an untrimmed beard and unruly black curly hair, all shot with gray.)

PABLO CORTEZ: Hi, everybody!

AP: Pablo, is this the way you usually dress while doing your splatterpainting?

PC: Naw, I usually wear less, but my mama taught me to dress when I get company.

AP: Would you like to say something to your mother?

PC: Sure would. Too bad it's impossible. She's dead. My father too. They fooled around with a lot of drugs in their time with one of those neo-Aztec cults. People keep saying that's why I survived my encounter with the Sirens.

AP: How interesting. Have drugs been an inspiration for your art?

PC: No! I don't believe it's necessary, especially with an imagination like mine.

AP: Do you use drugs recreationally?

PC: Not lately. Not after the Sirens. Sure, I fooled around with alk and canniboids—the usual kid stuff—when I was younger, but it was never more than a passing interest to me. Being drunk or stoned makes it hard to paint and draw—and *that's* the most important thing in my life!

(He starts looking at the paint-spattered canvas that lines the studio.)

AP: That puts you at odds with some of

the leaders of the System's art community.

PC: That doesn't bother me. I've always been at odds with communities. And leaders. I've always lived between worlds, never quite at home anywhere—but able to travel anywhere.

AP: And you certainly have traveled. You were born in the eastern sector of Los Angeles, orbited in Hightown, and ended up in the Jovian System.

(His eyes are still fixed on part of the canvas.)

PC: Uh, yeah ... I also bummed around the norteamericano continent back in my teens and early twenties—you know, cheap, obsolete vehicles-for-hire that were built back in the twentieth century that often left me and assorted campesinos and their pigs and chickens stranded way out in the middle of nadawhere. Still, I got to cross war zones, jungles, and deserts, see cities, murals, ruins, and museums, and find out how a big chunk of the human race still lives in this here new, improved twenty-first century. Quite an education, really.

AP: And yours has mostly been a do-it-yourself education. You don't have a high-school diploma and never went to college.

(He turns to look at her for a moment, then resumes contemplating the canvas.)

PC: I went to college—I just never bothered to register. I always figured the best way to approach schools was like a thief— or a Guerrilla Muralist—sneak in, ransack the place, satisfy a few curiosities and desires, then get the hell outta there before someone snaps the cuffs on you!

(He stretches his legs out to a wall, launches himself to the patch of canvas he's been looking at, and starts working it with his fingers. The camera tries to follow.)

AP: Did you get this attitude from your parents?

PC: No. They were college-educated Chicano intellectuals. Both had degrees in anthropology. The problem was they identified more with the people being studied than with the anthropologists. Probably what made them go neo-Aztec. They were working on an Aztec myth cartoon project. . . .

AP: Do you consider yourself anti-intellectual?

(He turns to her. The camera stays on the paint he is working.)

PC: No! I believe in the intellect, thinking, studying. I like intellectuals. It's *institutions* that I don't trust. Why is anybody who hasn't sold his brain to a bureaucracy and doesn't wait for official permits to think called anti-intellectual?

(He goes back to painting.)

AP: But since the arrest and disbanding of the Guerrilla Muralists of Los Angeles, you've had to deal with several institutions. . . .

PC: Yeah, but I dealt with them *my* way. Not like the rest of GMLA. Except for my buddy, Buck Waldo, they're still back in their hometown, waiting for committees to vote on their ideas before starting work.

AP: Let's talk about the Guerrilla Muralists of Los Angeles. Most of the System knows about them because of you, yet strangely they are relatively unknown outside of the L.A. sprawl. . . .

PC: They stood regional. Thought small. Didn't go nowhere.

AP: But how did the group form? How did you get involved with a group of art students?

Uh-oh. Here goes. Looks like I gotta do a verbal autobio—at the same time all these images on the canvas are getting ripe and near the danger point where the Sirenflashes'll fade and Willa'll have done something for nothing.

And the camera is moving in close to catch my fingers fondling the paint. No bother—I'm an exhibitionist, I don't mind an audience—in fact, I *love* an audience! And now I've got the whole System (or at least those plugging into II) looking over my shoulder. Yippie!

The part of my brain that handles talk is different from the part that does painting. I can do both modes at the same time. Just open up all the gates and let it all pour out!

I splat some more paint on Anna.

Let the show begin. . . .

# = 2 =
## GMLA

It all started one day when I had snuck into
the library of Cal State L.A., the place where
bright kids of the L.A. sprawl go once
they've exhausted the resources of their
friendly neighborhood community college—and they haven't become completely
disillusioned—and can't afford some big,
prestigious university. I literally bumped
into Estela Villanueva. . . .

FROM AN INTERVIEW WITH ESTELA
VILLANUEVA ON "EX-LOVES OF THE
RICH AND FAMOUS":
  (She is a slightly plump, striking Chicana
in her early thirties, conservatively made up
and dressed in California semiformal style.)
  ESTELA VILLANUEVA: I first met Pablo
when I was studying art at Cal State L.A.
We literally bumped into each other in the
library. I've always kind of suspected that
he did it on purpose. We were both carry-

17

ing heavy armloads of art books that immediately dumped on the floor. I was impressed with what he was carrying—books on surrealism, primitive and pre-Columbian art, abstract expressionism, Mexican muralists, late-twentieth-century graffiti art, recent works on the Space Culture Project. Then I got a good look at him: he definitely didn't look like a student, was a little older than average, wasn't wearing the latest uniform, but then he wasn't one for uniformity. He wore an eclectic mix of exotic, ethnic, surplus, and kitsch in a way that showed a strong sense of style. And that face—there's a famous piece of Aztec sculpture of the head of a warrior in an eagle helmet—he could have posed for it with his classic Aztec nose and cheekbones. His skin was this delicious reddish brown. His hair was a wiry black halo, and when he smiled, those killer dark brown eyes and that sensuous mouth framed by a thin mustache melted me.

. . . so I turned on the old Pablo Cortez charm, because, ay, she was caliente/picante with that long, straight, shiny black hair and that face that was too long and thin and not quite brown enough to be una India, but those cheekbones just had to be native to this continent. And her fine, firm chichis and nalgas showed their shape through that form-hugger student-chic pseudo-biz suit that she and all the niñas wore to college back in the twenty-twenties.

AP· Was that the early twenties or the late twenties?

PC: Early.

AP: Wasn't that about the same time the first Odysseus mission lowered a man into the Great Red Spot?

PC: Yeah, I was really interesado in it— those spectacular close-ups of Jupiter with all those warm-colored clouds swirling and not quite mixing—it was one of those things I talked to her about. That is, after I noticed that we had both dropped a lot of the same kind of art books all over the floor, figured this babe's got taste and maybe brains as well as chichis and nalgas, came up with a brilliant idea of starting a flirty argument about which books belonged to whom, soon we were talking up a storm. Somebody rudely told ūs to shut up, we decided to go out somewhere to suck some coffee—and soon we were a regular item!

EV: And turned out he wasn't a student. He'd just hang around, start talking to somebody in front of the library, and walk through the security check as their guest. He said they had one of the best collections of art books for miles around. He showed me this sketchbook full of the craziest drawings—wild stuff that often tore the paper in execution. I never saw such energy, but still they gave me some déjà vu. And he had such wide interests—he was all excited by the SCP and Odysseus One since the earlier detection of life-forms. He loved the possibility of seeing something he never saw before. And he had seen things, he'd traveled even though he had no money—he worked graveyard at a stop-and-rob wearing a protective vest, mask, and helmet. So different from the guys I was meeting at Cal. Especially the art crowd I hung out with. Seems he was always around me for the next few days. I remember we watched the coverage of the Odysseus One mission together, at my apartment.

FROM II'S COVERAGE OF THE ODYSSEUS ONE GREAT RED SPOT PROBE: (Open with an animated model of Jupiter and moons. Zoom in. The Great Red Spot fills the screen. Fade to studio set with II science correspondent Leon Wagner, wearing a stylized space suit. The Jupiter System model, fully animated, is blue-screened in the background.)

LEON WAGNER: Greetings, II-eyers! I'm sure all you lovers of science, beauty, and adventure will be fixed in front of your holo-systems for the next few hours, because Interplanetary Infotainment—the leading network of the Information Age—is bringing you live coverage of what may be humankind's first contact with extraterrestrial life-forms! I can't tell you how excited I am to be bringing this to you live, albeit time-lagged, from Ithaca Base, the self-contained mothership of Odysseus One, that has just been installed in a stable synchronous orbit over the Great Red Spot, making it the System's newest space colony, and humankind's furthest outpost in the universe!

(Fade to a view of Ithaca Base, a rotating wheel-type space station with a large propulsion unit that is being cannibalized into a power source.)

I imagine that the journalists of the twentieth century never dreamed that journalists of the twenty-first century would actually be going along on the exploration of space—but then they probably never dreamed of anything like the Sirens.

(Fade to a live view of the Great Red Spot, then to a cybermodel of Jove Diver.)

As we all remember, ten years ago, Jove Diver, an unmanned probe, a sort of combination of bathyscaphe and dirigible that could withstand the pressures of the Jovian atmosphere and float in it using tanks of lighter-than-Jupiter's-air gas. Some wondrous images were beamed back to us, and some data that has changed the scientific view of the universe—the discovery that most captured the public imagination—the presence of the Sirens . . .

(Fade in Leon Wagner, superimposed in front of the live view of the Great Red Spot.)

. . . microorganisms detected by Jove Diver in the atmosphere of Jupiter, and in greatest concentration, here in the Great Red Spot. These single-celled creatures interact with electrical activity that theorists compare to brain activity—for which the term "zapware" was coined. The scale on which zapware operates seems as large as the big planet itself; Jove Diver was overcome by Sirens, and its electrical systems were burned out. The scientific and public imaginations were enthralled; not only had we found life on another planet, but the slim hope of its being intelligent in some way.

(Fade to a rotating computer model of the Odysseus One dirigiscaphe.)

So now a new, larger—and manned—dirigiscaphe, with a gondola lined with the latest ultralightweight shielding to protect the "Sirenaut" from the deadly radiation of the Jovian System, the Odysseus One has been brought to the Jovian System, and tonight a man will be lowered into the Great Red Spot and attempt to communicate with the Sirens. . . .

EV: I mean, he was really into it. Intensely, in a way only he could be. It was the first time we were *really* going to get *intimate*, if you know what I mean, and his eyes—those dark, brown, almond eyes—got locked onto the screen. For once he was quiet, up to then he gave me a nonstop seductive babble, only shutting up when we were looking at some kind of art that he liked or when he drew something in that sketchbook for me. I was feeling a bit put off, I mean after the way he so passionately pursued me, *I* was expecting to be what those mad eyes were focusing on—but it was like he was trying to memorize every pixel of the images being broadcast from Jupiter. It was a little scary.

Mira, I'm an artist, a visually oriented person who thinks and lives and breathes images. I guess I fell in love with the big planet's looks early—those swirling warm-colored storm clouds seemed alive to me; they even influenced my early teenage painting style. There's something about the dynamic fractalized images of fluid mechanics that really gets to me. That first night in Estela's apt got me overloaded: the Odysseus coverage *and* this hot muchacha—ay! I thought that I just might die like my parents did from their ATL overdoses, but it would mean more pleasure than I had ever had before without slapping pigments around. I was game. Just like astronaut Phil Hagen was when they strapped him into the exoskeleton, sealed him into the dirgiscaphe, and lowered him away. . . .

TRANSCRIPT FROM SPACECO ODYSSEUS ONE MISSION:

ODYSSEUS ONE: Looks like I got a smooth fall here.

ITHACA BASE: Telemetry shows same, Phil. Retros sequencing smart. How's your exoization?

OO: I feel heavier, like during a lift, but I can move, just like wheel tests.

IB: You're zeroing on the Spot. Giving a spectacular view.

OO: Like a big red hurricane with no eye. Visual confirmation of lightning flashes. Scanners show area Siren-rich as usual. Contact is imminent. Have entered upper atmosphere. Flapchutes deployed.

EV: I was getting frustrated. Some teasing was in order. I leaned my head against his, breathed into his ear, tickled his chest, and said, "You watch all this sci stuff like you were some kind of techie."

He gave me one of those grunt/groans that I would soon know well, pointed to the screen, and said, "That is art."

Then he rolled up his left sleeve and showed me the tattoo. It was in big, black letters that ran back and forth from wrist to inner elbow joint spelling out: *Painting is not done to decorate apartments. It is an instrument of war for attack and defense against the enemy.—Pablo Picasso.*

"Where did you get that?" I asked.

"I did it myself with a felt-tip pen and safety pin in jail."

"When were you in jail?"

"Yeah, I've been un bad muchacho."

"Who is the enemy?"

"You know, they're all over, putting limits on what artists—all people—can do, trying to diminish the power of the imagination, censor our possibilities, cripple us all by widening the gap between the art of technology and the technology of art."

I laughed. " 'Art of technology and technology of art' . . . sounds like an old-fashioned corporate slogan."

"Shut up and let me watch this," he said, grim and distant.

So we watched it.


IB: Odysseus, do you read?

OO: Roger, base. Have entered the Spot. Gasbags sustaining flotation. Exoization fine. All indicators show area to be extremely Siren-rich. Electrical activity heavy.

IB: Any detectable patterns in the electri-cals?

OO: Seems heavier as the Sirens get thicker.

IB: Is there an increase in Siren-richness?

OO: Roger. They would appear to be swarming me.

IB: Watch for lightning effects on vehicle. Go for liftburn if it reaches danger level.

OO: Roger, base. But I really don't think that'll be necessary. I'm feeling fine. Just terrific. Great, in fact. Like the exoskeleton not only lets me move, but made all this big, bad heavy gravity go away. I'd swear I was in less than Earth-normal, almost like the rush of freefall.

IB: Phil, are you all right? You sound funny. Biotelemetry shows some off read-ings.

OO: Well, maybe you're experiencing a little instrumental failure there, boy. I tell you, I feel great, wonderful! The clouds . . . they seem to speed up . . . then go into slow motion . . . it's like I can feel them right through the vehicle . . . I know all this sounds impossible . . . but it's what I'm go-ing through here . . . like I'm floating . . . and it's all warm and comfortable . . . oh my! Would you look at all that! It's beautiful!

IB: All bioreadings at danger levels. Abort suggested.

OO: (white noise)

IB: Odysseus? Phil? Are you there? Abort! Abort! Remote override all systems! Escape boost burn now!

For one of the few times in my life, I was drained. Phil Hagen's death really got to me—everything, all thoughts and dreams and every bit of my big, gordo Pablo Cortez egoísimo seemed to leak out and leave me in a crumpled heap. I hadn't been affected by anything since that day when I was five that I woke up and wandered over to find Madre y Padre dead.

Funny, it wasn't because I felt much of anything about Phil Hagen—he was a typical nondescript astronaut—not even the fact that he was black and raised in Brazil made him much different from the sterilized whitebread spacemen of the mid-twentieth century. He was all hard-edge haircut and close shave all the way down to the convolutions of his brain. I can't even recall anything he ever said that interested me.

What he was, was my—and everybody else who was tuned in that night, and from what I remember it was most of the human race that could find a screen to look at—link with the outer edge of human experience. Through him we all got a strong taste of another world. It was strange, scary, and in the end deadly . . . but I was hooked.

* * *

EV: So there we were, both emotionally devastated—me a little more than him, having gotten a head start with his remark about art, the tattoo, and jail—with nothing to do but lean on each other. There was this long silence in which the holo went on and on without either of us seeing or hearing it while we held each other in this soft, melting way. When we finally did talk, it was after some of the most—uh—after we made love. I was amazed. I saw this side of him I never saw before. He had let his usual guard down, wasn't as frenzied, but was just as intense. I guess I really fell in love with him that night. I often wonder if he would have opened up to me that way if it wasn't for the death of Phil Hagen.

It was about four in the morning and neither of us could sleep. He got up and turned off the holo. I put on my robe, then put on some Chocholak-influenced music—but then what musician wasn't Chocholak-influenced in those days?—and went over to stare out the window. It was the familiar awful view of the complex's parking lot that I would often stare off into during moments of stress—same old walls, same old cars, same old graffiti . . . except for this one piece.

It glowed and spattered in a bold new style that my art-student friends and I no-

ticed and admired. It reminded me of something that I couldn't quite access at the
moment. There were these tangled, exploding letters over a rather realistic rendering
of a human heart. I concentrated and tried
to decipher the letters—at the same time
Pablo started looking at me, anxiously—
they spelled out my name: ESTELA.

Pablo smiled and said, "Oh, I see you
finally noticed my Aztec valentine to you."

Then she smiled all bright and cheerful—
the media-event death of Phil Hagen was
suddenly millions of light-years beyond her
sphere of concern—and mine too, actually.
We had retreated from the zapware dimension of modern history, back into our cozy,
merging personal lives. But at the same
time I expanded into something other than
some interesante guy that she was becoming involved with.

"You," she said, "you're the one who does
that great graffiti!"

"Yup," I said, "that's me." And that look
in her eyes told me that I could probably
talk her into just about anything. I was a
little disappointed.

EV: Naturally, I had to introduce him to
my friends. He was a hero because of his
bold style and the way he relentlessly put
his work out in front of the public. They

were just dying to meet him—and maybe even work with him. I don't think Pablo was very impressed with them. We were all students working inside the system, hoping to become artists—he was an artist, and he didn't need to ask anybody's permission. But he was rather lonely, living in that cheap one-room crackerbox in a converted freewayside motel with a lot of books and an ever-growing rat's nest of sketchbooks and artwork. There was this desperation—I could see it in those dark, almond eyes. He wasn't satisfied with the way his life was going, and did he ever want to go somewhere.

They were just a bunch of kids, still locked into formal education while I'd been Señor Hit-and-run since my early teens. I didn't seem like a student, so they treated me like a teacher—they couldn't help it, they hadn't learned to interact as equals yet. They weren't bad, were flirting with fashionable twenties artistic and political radicalism, knew all the slogans but didn't quite understand todos los ideas. Desiree and Jill were cute and full of fire. Maria was deep into televoodoo and totally bizarre. Johnny, LeRoy, and Moe had talent but weren't sure of themselves. Buck's techie skills were impressive, and he knew more about the SCP than me. An energetic bunch.

We did a lot of talktalktalk. I got tired of it, pronto.

EV: One time Pablo was just sitting around looking bored, then stood up and screamed, "Talk! Talk! Talk! You all sound like a bunch of student nadaheads! Let's do something!" There were some "oh yeah, like what?" statements batted around, and before we knew it, the Guerrilla Muralists of Los Angeles were formed.

They were suddenly all looking at me as their leader. It made me sick, but was a real lift. Suddenly I had a bunch of apprentices like the graffiti writers of old before the big legal crackdown of the nineties. And I was getting feedback, talking about my work to people who almost knew what it was about—which beat el infierno out of mediascanning until some feature or editorial about my work and how talented but misguided I was popped up. It was seductive. Like Estela.

EV: Buck offered to rig up a camera he was fooling around with—a cheap, low-fi kid's toy that he had modified—to record our first meeting. Pablo didn't like the idea, thought it could be used as evidence—he always thought like a criminal. Then Buck told him about the modifications—color switching, randomized autofocus, and that whole thing could be lightpainted over so it would look like cyberanimation. Pablo agreed, and suggested that we suspend the camera from a helium balloon, like a dirigiscaphe in the Jovian atmosphere.

FROM "GUERRILLA MURALISTS OF L.A. MEETING ONE," COURTESY OF THE SO-CAL BEAUTIFUL ARCHIVES:

(Camera comes on facing Buck Waldo, who's making a few adjustments before letting it fly.)

BUCK WALDO: We have go's all around. Let's do it.

PABLO CORTEZ: We gotta remember that all this meeting caca isn't an end in itself—it's just the preliminaries to doing something.

MARIA DAVIS: Isn't this doing something? What about televoodoo aesthetics? Are we gonna tear some holes in the telecom mythosystems, infecting the minds of the masses with mutagenic dreams, changing by manipulating the public imagery and releasing the lectronic loas?

PABLO CORTEZ: Mystometaphysical mumbo jumbo!

MARIA DAVIS: I'm talking techie! My kind of techie!

BUCK WALDO: Let's do something real.

PABLO CORTEZ: Let's do something, period! If all you muchachitos want to do is make homemade documentaries of yourselves, I'm out of here.

JOHNNY WU: Hey, we all wanna do something. The world is going crazy and it's spilling all over the solar system. Somebody's gotta do something.

JILL WAVERLY: I think our main problem is also the main problem of civilization: for us art has become so separated from life and living that it seems useless, but we still have the basic human need to use creativity as a survival tool, and if we don't, the evolutionary results could be disastrous.

DESIREE ORTEGA: (snoring noise) 'Scuse me, but why don't we just party?

MOE MORGAN: Jill does have a point, but I don't think we should get bogged down in intellectualisms. We have a lot to learn from Pablo. We also need to start making art matter again, by taking it out of the galleries and culture channels and putting it in front of everybody's face as they're going about their business!

PABLO CORTEZ: Yeah, we gotta *do* things.

ESTELA VILLANUEVA: You're already doing things, Pablo. You should tell us how you get your pieces done.

LEROY HILL: Yeah, man. How do you do those things?

PABLO CORTEZ: Well, I don't sit around in meetings talking about it. I just get an idea, decide where to do it, how to do it—then go out and do it!

MARIA DAVIS: Great—I could have said that.

BUCK WALDO: But you didn't, didn't you?

MARIA DAVIS: So what bright ideas do you have, techie boy?

BUCK WALDO: I think we should be an outlaw alternative to the regular art scene, which is still stuck back in the twentieth century. We should do stuff like what the SCP could do if it was set free in the streets.

MARIA DAVIS: The SCP? They just prop up all the same old official corporate myths!

BUCK WALDO: I meant the way they use new technologies in new ways.

PABLO CORTEZ: Yeah, I've been following their stuff for years. They kick some colas. Their stuff gives me a lot of graffiti ideas.

MOE MORGAN: So we got any more ideas?

JILL WAVERLY: This group has ideas dripping out of every pore.

ESTELA VILLANUEVA: So let's hear some.

DESIREE ORTEGA: And make it a party!

BUCK WALDO: Yeah, let's outdo the SCP!

* * *

The meeting tape was cute-ito. But it was more fun to be there and doodle all over it with the lightbrush than it was to watch. And these kids loved watching it. They made me sit through it too many times. I wished I'd burned it after a while.

EV: The meeting tape was our first group art project—it's still popular among art students—but it was the sort of thing that Pablo didn't appreciate. He was more interested in actually making art than talking about it, and once he did one project, he wanted to go on with another. He would only seem to be tired for a short period of time in between. Most of us needed to drink a lot of coffee, take caffeine tabs and even stronger stuff to keep up with him. He didn't even drink much socially. Art was his addiction.

Anyway, el groupo needed something to grab widescan media attention. Something big, monumental that could not be ignored. I suggested we do a monster-scale mural on some important public place, maybe even L.A.'s city hall. Then Buck Waldo came up with this outrageous idea for paint bombs. . . .

**PAN-SYSTEM NEWSERVICE DISPATCH:**
(LOS ANGELES) — This morning a three-

mile area around the Los Angeles Civic Center was painted orange. Police have found the self-destructed remains of what seem to be devices that sprayed out huge clouds of paint. The devices were placed during the predawn hours by a group calling itself the Guerrilla Muralists of Los Angeles, according to a manifesto sprayprinted on streets near the scene.

"We are putting art back into life where it belongs" was a key phrase in the rambling manifesto signed, simply, the Guerrilla Muralists of Los Angeles.

"They may be claiming to be artists," said L.A. Police Chief Abdul Acosta, "but they're vandals in my book. All this incident has resulted in is the damaging of public and private property, thousands of dollars' worth. I vow to find out who they are and make them pay."

Sure, the Oranging of L.A. was a dumb idea, but it was simple, and we could do it—pronto! I was sure that most of the Muralists were going to throw up before the bombs were placed, but somehow they managed to pull it off.

And you should have seen the way all these kids acted when the media reaction started to trickle in—you'd think we were a government watching the reviews of our latest microwar! We had a party at my place and the four generations of bikers living in the next room complained about the noise. You couldn't hear the freeway over the carrying on.

Still, this was just a warm-up. I wanted to get down to some real painting. . . .

EV: Even though he never really said so, Pablo was excited about everything the GMLA did, even when planning the Oranging he was excited, smiling, dancing around with nervous energy. He had been an artist all by himself until then—I was the first person he ever told about his graffiti activities—I guess he really liked me—but now he could actually share it with people, other artists. He was inspired, activated, and I think he really liked being a leader.

. . . and then one of them would call me their leader and I'd tell them never to call me that filthy word again. What a pile of freeze-dried caca! Then they'd all get a little quiet and hurt-looking, so I'd have to make some kind of joke and start talking about what the hell we were going to do next, and soon we were out there, decked out in gear that looked like cyberpunk nostalgia, attacking the blank/bleak wallspace of L.A.

ART REVIEW FROM THE *L.A. FREEBIE* BY NIGEL WELWORTH:

And they say that culture died back in the twentieth century! And they still call L.A. a cultural wasteland! Well, maybe that all might have been true before that magic morning when we all woke up to discover that the entire civic-center area had turned bright orange. The Big Orange suddenly really was—simply marvelous! The act/event/ work was so pure, so perfect, that it would have been more than enough for it to have been an end in itself, but no, lucky for the SoCal aesthetic scene, there was more, the Guerrilla Muralists of Los Angeles Manifesto!

Now, being in the ArtCritBiz as long as I have, I've seen most of the manifestos issued so far in the 21st century—some of them showed promise and others were just plain boredom city. This one was a serious standout in that from the very first it was backed up by action and concrete reality. The civic center was—and still is—glowing bright orange through the smog for godsake.

The GMLA has put "art back into life where it belongs" and made it "inescapable, lurking all over the sprawl, zapping brains like televoodoo virus programs, cracking mindsets and altering viewpoints as biz goes on as a bit unusual after a while."

For the first time in the seventeen years

since I installed myself in L.A., doing the freeway flux is a regular pleasure. I watch the traffic till I'm driving on spinal memory and the eyes relax into not seeing—then something knocks 'em back into action! Color has erupted in the night on some plain, drab concrete (or worse, pastel-painted concrete) and lively provocative images mind-rape me: happy commuters smile at me from some utopian masstrans system painted on a freeway retaining wall; familiar landmarks get lost in gleaming jungle foliage and are attacked by ancient sci-fi monsters; soldiers and war machines flood the suburbs; starving hordes beg with sad eyes, open hands, and distended bellies; zombies take over office buildings turned into graveyards; Quetzalcoatl chokes on smog; an electrified Eurzulie conjures public orgies; Uncle Sam holds up the heart of a draftee to the gaping jaws of a biomechanoid war god; and electronic loas dance on satellites . . . televoodoo virus programs indeed!

And it's not just trendy twenty-first-century visual reunited with the literary. No official neoillustratoids here. The style is bright and frantic, splattery—suggesting some industrial multipaint guns with cyber-aided color mixing and switching capabilities as well as adjustable spray nozzles adapted for maximum expressive possibili-

ties, allowing complex painting to be created at high graffiti speed; because these
murals are big and elaborate, they must be
done fast so's they are finished and the
Guerrilla Muralists are miles away by the
time the police can respond to their expensive scanstuff and get there to see the latest
masterpiece.

Makes me start feeling that maybe there's
some hope for this here sprawl short of
tact-nuke urban renewal.

Then I get to the gallery, museum, or lo-
cation of the show or event I'm supposed to
review and I'm usually bored into a near
coma.

Oh well, it's a living. I guess.

. . . and after that rave review from Welworth in the *Freeb*, it was mass mental orgasm time. Loco ecstasy all aroundo. We
were all big chingón artists, modern ver-
sions of neolithic shamans putting magic
images on the closest things we had to cave
walls, or televoodooist houngans, "giving
shock treatments to the Systemic electromagnetic hive-mind, programming new
kinds of loas to slip into every media-
deadened head and jolt the zombies into
fighting to win back their own minds like
Nuke Damballah said in that interview the
other day," as Maria would lecture us. We'd
talk about how what we were doing was go-

ing to change the world, then check out a
tape of some new documentary about our
work:

"Something new under the L.A. smog . . ."

"The work of a new kind of urban genius
spawned by the multicultural tensions of
SoCal . . ."

"Desperate cries in the wilderness of contemporary alienation."

"Another reason to leave California."

"Another reason to live in California."

"Another reason that California is California."

You get locoized in the cabeza with that
sort of stuff after a while. I was always con-
vinced that I was destined to be a great artist
that was going to shake up el todo mundo. I
don't know, maybe it's all my parents' fault
with their neo-Aztec ATL fantasies of bringing a new Quetzalcoatl into the world.


EV: We were partying, celebrating putting diabolical robot centipedes (Pablo's
idea) around some fat, freeway pillars,
swilling some cheap generic beer and listening to Tex Toyota and the Samurai Cow-
girls' big hit album when Maria brought out
some party canniboid—you know, that stuff
recomboed to increase social skills and ver-
balization—from inside her embroidered
Nigerian dance jacket.

"Lookie hear," she said. "Got some good-ies that'll make us one with the loas!"

We all cheered, but I noticed that Pablo got all ice-faced.

Maria loaded a little pipe shaped like a coiled snake, said, "Ready to zap them syn-apses," and took a long, lusty suck, then passed it around. We all had a lungful—me too—and soon were feeling witty and laser sharp and talking madly, not really both-ering to listen to each other; we were hav-ing too much fun.

But Pablo didn't have any.

When it got passed to him, he turned it down, saying, "I don't need it."

"I think you do," said Desiree. "You aren't being very sociable."

"Don't give me that game," he said. "I got over the need to be like anybody's crowd years ago. I don't need it. I don't want it. Just leave me alone."

And he went off by himself. I followed and asked, "Anything wrong?"

"No. Nothing really. It's just that I have this thing about drugs, playing with them. My parents, they were neo-Aztecs and they died when I was five from an ATL overdose. I toddled into their room and found them."

"Atl?"

"A-T-L. A word meaning 'water' and a common syllable in the language of the Az-tecs. It was also an old NASA term for Advanced Technology Lab. It was actually recomboed organic hallucinogens."

"I'm sorry. I didn't know."

"It wasn't your fault—it was theirs."

"Wasn't it supposed to cause genetic mutations?"

"That was a myth. There's been no documented proof of that. And I don't want to talk about it and me and how I got this way. I heard it all before, and I'm sick of it."

"Okay," I said, and snuggled up to him. He snuggled back. . . .

After a while we reentered the party. Moe was complaining about kids putting graffiti on our murals.

"Let 'em," Pablo said. "We made our mark . . . nothing lasts forever anyway."

Nobody could figure out what he meant— until later.

I don't know, just must be the way I am. Hey, maybe there was something about ATL causing mutations, or maybe it's because I was raised neo-Aztec in a relocated barrioid then ended up in a paleofuturoid instant suburb fighting a psychwar with the melting pot upwardly mobile SoCal zombies. Hell, I never had a microchancito of being anybody's kind of normal. I'm the universal heathen, outside of all boundaries; so when you get me in a group of any kind for any amount of time, I start pacing the floor, climbing the walls, and checking out where the exit is.

In my L.A. graffiti phase I was el lone lobo howling without anybody on my side—then kerblamo! I got this muchacha bella and am being treated like a heroísimo by a bunch of crazy kids with a little talent and a lot of energy. Ése, that's real dangerous—muy peligroso!

The murals we did were great, brimming over with clashing styles and ideas—it's incredible that we got anything done! They all thought we invented the wheel or something. It was all some sort of adventure in the lowlife for them—a bunch of students who were used to flying Trans Mid-Class—and I'd been down and dirty, close to the asphalt, and coated in smog for some time.

There were a lot of hideous realities slithering around that they never dreamed of or would ever be ready for. . . .

EV: Maybe I never really understood Pablo. I thought he'd get behind Moe in wanting to clash with the local gang graffiti writers over their scribbling on our murals. I don't know, I guess I figured that being so . . . earthy and really into the old-fashioned Chicano things that he'd have all kinds of macho obsessions. I was afraid he'd want to lead us into gang warfare. . . .

I was afraid. I grew up hooked to a stereo-video system, commuting from suburban family condo to mall. I couldn't speak Spanish if my life depended on it. And he had been places, was so sure of himself, and looked like he was capable of violence.

But if he did lead us into a gang war, I would have followed. And so would the others.

I had my share of brushes with local gangs—they're like local police or government, only not as easy to deal with. Wherever you go, you gotta deal with whoever thinks they're the head chingón—usually by steering clear, if not playing dumb. If that doesn't work, play it smart. If that doesn't work, you gotta fight—either spook 'em or nuke 'em.

The graffiti issue is usually simple—I'd just leave 'em some negative space to go put their names in and not complain about my work being defaced when I'm in the defacing business myself.

Then there's the real criminals. The junior mob. Los pachucos nuevos of every race, creed, and color that stake out some minuscule slice of the worst living space around, announce it to whoever else that's stuck there, and proceed to make things miserable until usually they and a lot of other people end up as bloody corpses.

That's why when I was working in that

East L.A. stop-and-rob I'd wear that helmet, mask, and armor—not to be trendy like the clerks in fashionable max-security boutiques, even though I'd painted crude skeletal designs on mine—more psychological warfare than high fashion. This place got hit regularly, but not constantly, and usually there'd be no violence—just toss 'em a little dinero and they'd run. Then most nights it'd be nadaland on the graveyard shift; customers were few and far between in the predawn hours, so I'd take a sketchbook and do some inspired doodling to keep me from dozing.

That's what I was doing the night that gaudy crookito in a tacky artificial feathered suit sashayed in with two hulking thugs in tow. He looked familiar; I'd seen him on the streets and interviewed on a local news show. He leaned over and tapped my gauntlet with his gold-tinted three-inch-long, metalized, razor-edged nails, then raked his claws across the fresh crayon smears on my sketchbook, scoring the paper, then smiled with fluorescent-capped teeth, fashionable as his glowshades, lightning-bolt lipstick, and featherish haircut dyed to match his suit.

I gave him the usual "May I help you, sir," knowing that this was not biz as per usual.

"You don't know who I am, ése?"

"Yeah, I know. You're the leader of Los

Boy Killers—Quetzalpilli. Your name means 'Feathered Prince' in Nahuatl."

"You know some Aztec talk. You're a smart one."

"My parents were neo-Aztecs. Nahuatl is almost a third language to me."

"Ay, ése," he said, smiling with more confidence than his scrawny, disnourished body should have been able to muster. "It is me y mis amigos"—the thugs hulked closer and flexed muscles hidden by bulky fascist-chic sport clothes that bristled with macho/hardware jewelry, some of which I recognized as being real, functional weaponry—"who can help you."

I tongued the ready switch in my mask, activating the store's defense system, praying that Huitzilopochtli was being a good war god and would make the gadgets work when I needed them.

This action was countered by small flashing lights in the thugs' goggles. They cleared their throats like stereo samurai.

The feather prince then picked up my sketchbook and handed it to a thug, who flipped through it for him. "Hey, not bad, ése. You are a muy talented muchacho. Some of this stuff looks a lot like some of the stuff that's been on a lot of SoCal walls. . . ." He scratched the sketchbook and threw it, knocking over a pyramidal display of fruit-flavored fungisnack cubes. "Including some of *my* walls."

The gold razor nails raked my mask, dancing around the eye screens.

"That, amigo, is not bueno. How can I control my streets when you mess up my walls—you never even asked? Now, I am a reasonable man. I know that la policía are after your nalgas for not asking their permission—un problema I have myself. I think what we need is un poquito cooperation here. Comprende, ése? Mis muchachos and I would gladly keep la policía away from you, if you would just make a dealito—say, from now on you *only* paint on *my* walls, and before you do, you come to mi casa and we talk, and you work out how to make your pictures get my message across—tell the people who runs this place, and what they gotta do to keep our protection . . . and what will happen to them if they don't!"

The same old line. Everybody wants to buy your talents for some sleazy need of theirs, and usually they don't even offer a good price.

Why do they always assume it's *me* that's for sale?

I was about to lick the fire switch when he said, "Mis muchachos smell some kinda defense system in here that's all warmed up and ready to go. That why they aimed their pistolas at you."

Their bulky, face-crusher gauntlets were facing me, heavy metal gloves with gleaming gun muzzles like extra sets of knuckles.

"You wouldn't want to do anything estúpido. . . ."

I licked the switch. People are always calling me estúpido.

The store's floor, except for the section behind the counter, was suddenly electrified, sending the guys hopping around locoísimo as the gas that was guaranteed to make thieves sick but not pollute the merchandise flooded the aisles. I sealed my mask, started sucking the stale air supply, when the glove guns went off.

I heard things shatter, fall, and sharp impacts on the suit, helmet, and chest plate that went through me like I was made of wet Kleenex. Then I felt all torn and splattery. Then I woke up in the hospital.

## FROM PABLO CORTEZ HOSPITAL-ROOM SURVEILLANCE TAPE:

(Alphonse Tanaka, a small Japanese man with thinning, gray hair enters the room.)

ALPHONSE TANAKA: Hello, Pablo. How are you feeling?

PABLO CORTEZ: Not as awful as yesterday. Still hurts. So what brings you away from your business to see me, jefe?

AT: Well, I was concerned. . . .

PC: About who?

AT: I have something to talk to you about.

PC: What, señor?

AT (pauses, looks at the camera): You know how it is. When something like this happens to a business. The store's all I've got, Pablo. Things could happen.

PC: So . . .

AT: I don't think it would be a good idea for you to work for me anymore.

PC: For who?

AT: Pablo, I really don't want to do this to you, but things could happen.

PC: Sure.

AT: Besides, you're an intelligent young man—talented too. You shouldn't be working in a store like mine. You should go back to school, try to make something of yourself. Why, with a little effort you could sign up with a good company and make real money.

PC: Sure.

AT (takes an envelope out of his pocket, hands it to Cortez): Here, to help you get going.

(Cortez takes the envelope in his hand, makes a fist, crumpling it.)

EV: I don't think I ever cried so much. Things were so wonderful there for a while—then . . .

When I found out, I rushed to the hospital. That was back when they were putting all that security on violent-crime victims: phone taps, metal detectors on the door, chemical sniffers, and video recording of whatever goes on in the room. They almost didn't let me bring in the sketchbook and crayons I brought for him.

Once I got in, we just looked at each other for a long time. We knew the authorities would be going over everything we did and said.

FROM PABLO CORTEZ HOSPITAL-ROOM SURVEILLANCE TAPE:

PABLO CORTEZ: Come over here, beautiful, I need a kiss.

(Estela Villanueva runs to the bed, puts her package on Pablo Cortez's lap, and leans over to kiss him.)

ESTELA VILLANUEVA: You hurt bad, baby?

PC: Naw, just some nasty bruises. The suit worked fine. It's the side effects that are killing me.

EV: Side effects?

PC: My boss, Señor Tanaka, fired me. Nothing personal, it's his policy—especially if the incident is gang-related. Doesn't want a repeat performance.

EV: You've got a lot going for you, Pablo. Another job should be no problem. You shouldn't have to work in places like that anyway. With your talent . . .

PC (gestures to the camera): Estela, cuidado . . .

EV (starting to cry): Damn. This is such a bitch. I'm so worried about you.

(They embrace again.)

PC: I missed you, querida. Feels a lot better having you here.

EV: Was there any serious damage?

PC: Naw, I should be outta here in a day or so.

EV: That's great. What about the (pause) our friends? You want them to come see you?

PC (gestures to camera): I don't think it'll be necessary. We can all talk after I get out. It won't be long.

(She kisses him again. Grabs the bag and gives it to him.)

EV: I brought you something.

(He pulls a sketchbook and box of crayons from the bag.)

PC: Hey, just what I've been begging for—besides you.

FROM THE POLICE ANALYSIS OF THE PABLO CORTEZ HOSPITAL-ROOM SURVEILLANCE TAPE:

After the visit from his girlfriend, in which she gave him a blank artist's sketchbook and a box of children's crayons, the subject proceeded to compulsively fill the pages of the sketchbook with strange, crude drawings.

A psychological adviser found similarities in the drawings to those made by institutionalized psychotics.

An art adviser found similarities in the drawings to certain local graffiti styles and the work of the Guerrilla Muralists of Los Angeles.

Further observation of the subject may be in order.

EV: When he got out of the hospital, I talked him into moving in with me. He was tired, desperate, scared, and paranoid. He'd draw restlessly, stopping regularly to check to see if anyone was watching him. Most of the time he didn't notice me; it was anything but romantic.

He told me, "I always act this way after a brush with death and/or authority," and tried to make a joke of it, then withdrew back into his frantic little world.

I told him not to worry about the future, offered to support him, even if I had to drop out of school. He could work on his art, maybe even try to sell some of it.

He just laughed and said, "That wouldn't work. Things are all fluxed up, changing around. I think they're closing in on me. The enemy." He rubbed his tattoo. One of these days I was going to gather up the nerve to ask who the enemy really was. "I just have to stay on the move, get some work done. Hey! Think I'll call the whole GMLA—get a meeting going. We gotta do something, a big projectísimo!"

They were all glad to see me. The guys all hugged me and pounded my back, the girls all kissed me—hell, Maria even slipped me a little tongue and I was sure she was a confirmed lesbo. I peeled off my shirt to show the fading bruises to the ooh-ah chorus, and when the emotional energy was at the right pitch, critical mass was achieved and we dreamed out loud, live and high-powered, we came up with El Último—the Guerrilla Mural to end all Guerrilla Murals. Of course, we didn't know it would be the end of the Guerrilla Muralists as well.

We were riding high on the adrenaline and beta endorphins—the others smoked some widewake weed, but I abstained—as we got ready like a team of ninja astronauts in surplus/obsolete gear that Buck had picked up—they were *giving* the stuff away—and adapted for our purposes: cat vision goggles; respirators to keep the paint out of our lungs; black, hooded protective coversuits and smart rainbow guns hooked up to our belts of paint cans. Then we piled into Johnny's megavan and shot up the nearest on ramp into the most convenient artery of the L.A. sprawl's legendary freeway system.

A lot of what we had done before was viewable from the freeways, because we saw the commuting millions as our prime audience. Nigel Welworth and other critics were calling it Freeway Art and even the official artisans of the SoCal Beautiful government arts project were getting in on it—soon everything in eyescan of the freeways that wasn't covered up by state-of-the-art billboards would be painted over in the pretentious name of Art. Ay, it made me sick in my panza! Well, what we were going to do this time was to take Freeway Art ahead one more stepísimo—instead of painting around the freeway, we decided to paint the freeway itself!

Yup, right on the lanes—so they'd only be able to be properly viewed from passing aircraft—we proceeded to put renderings of people—lots of people—and animals, all on a ground of lush vegatoid jungle symbols. A painted paradise that would be rapidly destroyed by the vehicles that passed over it every day.

Painting it was pure joy, a magic dance to Nuke Damballah's "Televoodooizing" in the dark by black-shrouded ghosts in a mist of paint spray.

"LOOK OUT! WE BE TELEVOODOOIZ-ING!"

It was Nuke's latest rapid-fire, heart-monitor drumbeats, rough-hewn rattle-tat-tattle—

"WE TELEVOODOOIZING AW NITE 'N AW DA DAY!"

—all bubbling out of shape through time-distorting synthatronics of some lectronic loa machine making our perfect sound track.

"TELEVOODOOIZING LECTRONIC LOAS DEEP INTA YA HEAD!"

The kids had learned my high-speed, hit-and-run spray style well.

"TELEVOODOOIZING YA OUTTA MEDIA-ZOMBIE SLEEP!"

Now and then a footprint would soil the living composition, only to be instantly made part of it all.

"TELEVOODOOIZING JU-JU/GRIS-GRIS INTA DA SYSTEM'S SATCOM NET!"

It was all going down beautiful and muy pronto—

"TELEVOODOOIZING FLUX-SOUNDS TA MUTATE AW YO DREAMS!"

—we were almost ready to hop back into the megavan and jet when that fat spotlight fell on us.

"TELEVOODOOIZING'S GONNA RE-ARRANGE YO GENES!"

Overhead a police whispercopter was coming down.

"TELEVOODOOIZING'LL REVOLU-TIONIZE ALL DA WORLDS!"

We were told not to move.

"WE TELEVOODOOIZING—YA GOTTA DO IT, TOO!"

Some tasteful warning shots were fired.

"TELEVOODOOIZING!"

The gunfire must have jolted me. I started to run. Maybe all this was televoodooizing.

"TELEVOODOOIZING!"

Like Nuke Damballah said, "Sometimes ya don't know why da loas makes ya do what ya do."

"TELEVOODOOIZING!"

There was some screaming. My fellow, loyal Guerrilla Muralists—those nutty, loyal revolutionaryoid kids who were will-ing (they said) to follow me to some glorious, living-color, fully holographied, prime-time martyrdom: "Don't move!" "Pablo, are you crazy!" "Stop!" "They're going to . . ."

"TELEVOODOOIZING!"

They—the LAPDers in the whispercop-ter—dropped a seizurizer that started its light/sound/sparkpulse show and we were all soon having induced epileptoid fits all over our latest work.

PAN-SYSTEM NEWSERVICE DISPATCH: (LOS ANGELES) — The Guerrilla Muralists of Los Angeles were arrested at 3:08 A.M. today while painting a section of the San Bernardino Freeway.

The GMLA turned out to be a group of local art students led by a nonstudent who the police were watching after his recent involvement in a gang-related shooting.

"Looks like a case of good but misguided kids led astray by a questionable character," commented Police Chief Abdul Acosta. "And not a moment too soon, either. Who knows what they'd have done if they were left running loose much longer. The taxpayers really got their money's worth for all of the department's state-of-the-art surveillance equipment on this one."

Due to the complicated legal nature of the arrest, the identities of the Muralists and the charges will be announced in a special media conference later today.

EV: I was terrified. Sure, I had my share of brushes with the police when I was in my teens—but I was never actually arrested. I was in quite a panic.

Then I talked to Jill, whose father was a lawyer. She calmed me down a bit. Then they never could come to a decision on exactly what to charge us with. Just a graffiti rap seemed like much ado about nothing after Chief Acosta made such a big deal about getting us, then we had become popular

SoCal heroes with all kinds of fans and admirers. Nigel Welworth had even started a Free the Muralists movement.

The only thing Acosta could do was to try to build Pablo up as some kind of lowlife boogeyman who corrupted us clean-cut, idealistic students.

It didn't help that Pablo was acting weird. . . .

It was desperado time for me. No job, sponging off Estela, in jail, not knowing how I was going to pay the hospital bills from the shooting . . . gimme a break, I had reasons.

I was sure they were watching me since I got out of the hospital. I think I even saw them a few times. I should have known better when we planned the freeway thing, but it felt so good to be doing something on that grande scale. Ay! Maybe I wanted us to get caught. Maybe I just saw this crazy group coming to a logical conclusion. It couldn't possibly go on forever.

EV: But it all ended up working to our advantage. People thought he was Van Gogh, Picasso, and Robin Hood rolled into one. The fact that all he did most of the time was watch TV shows on the growing interest in life on Jupiter, the SCP—he especially liked a sculptress named Firedrop—

and scribble frantically and mumble inscrutably only helped the myth grow. Welworth and others built him up into the great L.A. sprawl genius they were all waiting for.

Still, he didn't talk much to anybody.

Including me . . .

Finally, they brought us all into this office with a crowd of official-looking typísimos in suits and ties—there was even a judge! They wanted to make some kind of deal to make us pay for all the damage we did to public and private property and force us to learn respect for bureaucracy and filling out all the right forms and avoid a trial that would make all look bad during an election year.

Nigel Welworth walked up and introduced himself, said we had nothing to worry about. I wished he didn't sit so close to me.

Then the judge started talking. Ay, I thought we took the wrong elevator and ended up in another dimension. She said this was all off the record, informal, an out-of-court deal. Then she hit us with a load of bullcaca about how we were all such intelligent, talented young people— the hope of tomorrow, credits to our various races, blahblahblah—and she understood that some of us were from underprivileged backgrounds or alienated by sprawl life; still we did wrong in not going through the proper channels and we owed society something for it; but not to make us think that society was disapproving, or discouraging our artistic expression. . . .

Instead of going to trial and possibly to jail, the SoCal Beautiful public arts and decoration project had agreed to take us on as volunteer artists for a probation period after which we might even become full employees. All we had to do was officially disband the GMLA and promise never to engage in such illegal activities again.

Everybody sounded relieved and made approving noises.

Except me.

I then raised my hand and said, "Uh, your honor, this all sounds fine; but could we do our volunteer work for some other organization, if we feel we'd be more effective there?"

There were shocked and puzzled looks all around.

"Well, Mr. Cortez," the judge said, "we had been talking exclusively to SoCal Beautiful and they are enthusiastic about working with all of you."

"I'm sure they are, but I'm not sure I could work well with them—judging from the nature of their existing works . . . I'm not sure if I'd fit there. However, there are other organizations. . . ."

"What do you have in mind, Mr. Cortez?"

"Could you sign me up with the Space Culture Project? I mean, with me off planet, you won't have to worry about me messing up your walls."

"The SCP?" said Buck. "Me too! Me too!"

"Yeah, Buck here is my main tech adviser. I wouldn't think of spacing out without him."

"We've been fantasizing about this for some time now," said Buck.

The judge smiled and said, "We'll see if they'll have you, Mr. Cortez. And you too, Mr. Waldo."


EV: I was so relieved when I realized we weren't going to jail or even on trial. Then Pablo opened his mouth and I slid down the other side of the emotional roller coaster.

He hadn't even thought of me. Just all of a sudden he wants to go into outer space. I was choking back tears all the way to the party that Nigel Welworth was throwing for us. Pablo ignored me and jabbered to Buck about how they were going to rearrange Hightown with exploding paintings and free-wandering cyber/roboart monster machines.

He didn't even acknowledge me until he

accidently bumped into me while going for another beer.

I bumped into her while doing a más cerveza trot. She called me a bastard.

"Probablemente," I said. "I never was sure if my parents were legally married. All they did was some neo-Aztec ceremony."

Suddenly those dainty fistitos were pounding me. I bear-hugged her and dragged her outside.

She whined about how I'd been so cold to her for so long, and since I moved in—I only noticed her when I wanted sex and now I want to go off to Hightown when things started going good again.

What could I do? It was all true. I did a gulpísimo and let her have it with my side.

"Look, Estelita, I never wanted to form any revolutionary art gang and get into all kinds of trouble. That was all something you dragged me into, because you wanted to show me off to your friends. All I wanted from you was a bit of good, honest romance; some tenderness and juicy amor on lonely nights. I'm good enough at getting into trouble on my own."

"But you love it. All this attention, and the fact that you're going places now. You love it more than you ever loved me."

* * *

EV: Then he got this smug look on his face, looked me right in the eyes with that deadly intense stare of his, and said, "Yeah, I guess you're right."

I just collapsed. He saw that he could crush me and did.

After locking myself in the bathroom for a long, painful cry, I left the party, went home, and wished that the SCP would reject him, humiliate him ... but of course, they didn't.

The SCP was glad to take Buck and me. "We at the Space Culture Project feel honored that the two of you want to work with us." Seems they were always on the scan through the networks for local heroes, and we were prime candidates. "We've been watching the GMLA for quite a while now, and the two of you are obviously the prime catalysts of that group." They told us they wanted to "incorporate the latest innovations and subcultural influences into the space culture matrix."

Man, we were flying long before we got near any rockets!

"Yeah, we're going," I told Buck once we got out of the overairconditioned office and back onto the good, old, dirty-aired street.

"Soon we'll be on a Supershuttle," Buck said, arcing his hand like a launch vehicle.

One of my favorite visual puns popped into my head. "Ever notice how the vapor trail of a spaceship looks like a feathered serpent?"

Buck pulled his hand out of orbit. "You handing me some used ancient astronauts?"

"Naw, just some synchronicity. Like the Aztec poem that goes:

> *"Is it true that one lives only on Earth?*
> *Not forever on Earth: only a short*
> *    while here.*
> *Even jade will crack,*
> *Even gold will break,*
> *Even quetzal feathers will rend,*
> *Not forever on the Earth: only a short*
> *    while here."*

Poor Buck looked un poquito startled. "That poem about space travel?"

"No, actually it's about death."

He shuddered. "You get scary at times, Pablo."

EV: The funny thing is that it all worked for the best. Maybe Pablo knew it would, and that we were from different parts of the Chicano galaxy.

I really enjoyed working with SoCal Beautiful. They spotted my knack for organization, so soon I moved up into a position of authority and power. I like having a job and an organization to work with. I also think that our projects help make the L.A. sprawl a better place to live.

And I enjoy an affluent life-style. It's what I grew up with. I never was very happy trying to be a bohemian.

Now I'm married to Senator Fields, we have two wonderful children and a big, beautiful house. I don't think Pablo could ever live this way.

But that night when I saw the newsflash of him and Buck being accepted by the SCP, my heart broke. Then there was a piece on how II and Spaceco were negotiating to sponsor more Odysseus missions to encounter the Sirens and were getting lots of volunteers even though it would mean most of them would probably die. The idea of Pablo finding out about that scared me.

... come on, Anna! Ask me something else, move this on. This talk about Estela is triggering memories and emotions that the Sirens are dredging up into holo-hallucinations that are making all kinds of Willa pressures close in on me. And this is all taking me away from that blob of paint over there on that splotch that is just beg-

ging me to make it into a scene from a
world I don't know the first kinda nada
about. There! The splotch is now spread,
the scene takes shape, and I see Willa looking out at me. Finally Anna opens her
mouth. . . .

# = 3 =

## Hightown

Like I said, I've moved around the Mudball
before, but the trip to Hightown was a muy
grande skullopener. I was used to low-tech
obsolete outlaw travel—then here I am
checking into LAX West, or Wet, depending
on how the artificial island's floats were
holding out; getting my possessions deep-
scanned, talking to holocyberreceptionists,
zipping down tubewalks, listening to the ul-
traslow, deep drum music of lifting spacecraft; remembering when the sight of a
rickety, windowless, rust-coated methane
bus with clackety homemade wooden tires
made me feel that I was free at last! But
this was the century two-one the way it was
spozed to be—all gleaming and high energy
brimming with the buzzing rhythms that
could take you to the stars!

Buzz was acting like he was in his own
kind of paradise. I had to keep grabbing
him to keep him from trying to take things

apart for some creative cannibalization. We did this heavy nonstop crosstalk that drove everyone but us crazy, which suited us just fine because we were two hombres out to show the mundo what it's all gonna be!

And when we finally got to our Supershuttle, I really had to hold him back—he wanted to leap through the windows to get at it.

FROM A "SYSTEM ART WEEK" INTERVIEW WITH BUCK WALDO:

(Waldo is older in this recent interview, hair longer, with a full beard and contact lenses instead of his former trademark thick glasses.)

WALDO: I couldn't wait to get into that Supershuttle. Pablo had to hold me back and point out that I was attracting the shaded eyes of Spaceport Security. So we went into a talk fantasy about how we were going to take over Hightown—something we'd been practicing for the last couple of weeks until people were glad to see us leave. By the time we boarded I was in extracurricular need of being strapped in. When we lifted off ... Pablo and I shut up.

We had to. We were overwhelmed, crushed by the G-forces—out of the window I could see Pablo's feathered-serpentish vapor trails—then the freefall float set in and—well, was a little more meaningful stereo silence combined with paralysis that tried to resist the sudden lack of gravity, but you know how the muscles soon relax, the body seems to melt, and when it just don't go away, you know that this ain't no roller-coaster ride and, yup, you're inside outer space, all right, because you can feel it—you're floating.

I went into an idea blaze—figuring what it would be like to live and work in freefall, what kind of tech art I could do in this new environment. Then I glanced and saw Pablo fooling with a drinkbag; tossing, catching, observing the way the liquid moved while weightless—then he pinched open the nipple, squeezed a little Bud out, catching the golden, wobbly spheres on his fingers, drawing some glyphoids on his traytable, grabbing the drinkbag as it hit him in the face; taking it and squeezing more beer out, he said, "Jackson Pollock shoulda been an astronaut," and swatted it with his finger, sending beer blobs all over himself, me, the ceiling, a few other passengers, and especially the back of the seat in front of him where his vision was fixed.

Yeah—it happened right before my eyes, Pablo's invention of splatterpainting, and my microcam was tucked away in the overhead, so that great moment in art history just went right on by.

And a stewardess flung herself over and told him, "Would you please stop that, sir!"

FROM AN II "STATE OF THE ARTS" INTERVIEW WITH PERCIVAL WAGSTAFF, HIGHTOWN DIRECTOR OF THE SPACE CULTURE PROJECT:

(Wagstaff is tall, painfully thin, with his hair dyed a dull gray, and skin treated to have a corpselike pallor.)

WAGSTAFF: Well, my first impression of the two of them—I met them as part of a courtesy gesture from SCP—was that they were both rather attractive young men. And neither of them looked like artists—Cortez looked like a Mexican hoodlum with that wild hair and mustache spilling down to his chin; and Waldo looked like some kind of technician with simple haircut and those thick, old-fashioned glasses. Still, they were a pair of sexy young things.

I pegged them both for hopeless heteros by the way they flinched from my hugs and didn't return my kisses—even though I was sure they were warned. It didn't matter to me; despite some of the nasty rumors you may hear, I do not run a casting couch, and my interest in them was purely professional. Besides, I've had a happy, monogamous relationship for years; Raymundo and

I were of the first couples to be married in Hightown.

They simply brimmed over with energy and immediately began to talk my ears off with more ideas than my poor old brain could sort out all at once.

I made them an appointment to formally present these ideas before the SCP board and told them that they were welcome additions to our staff of artists, reminded them that the Hightown Culture Festival was coming up in a couple of weeks, and advised that they get themselves settled in soon.


"This ain't gonna be easy," I told Buck as we walked away from Wagstaff. "Not all the natives are nonhostilitos."

He more or less agreed with me, but said it probably wouldn't be so bad, that most of the SCP stuff we'd seen coverage of looked good—Fujimoto's prismatic laser environments, Arkov's floating canvases, Lorenzo's cyber/robo performances, Firedrop's freefall sculptures—that we'd at least be in good company.

Yeah, but there was something about that Wagstaff guy and his zombie looks—not to mention that he was an obvious maricón—that bothered me. . . .

Not that I'm a homophobe—I used to live in Mexico City near La Zona Rosa and just before spacing out I lived in the L.A. sprawl. I don't care how someone else chooses to get his dulces—just as long as they don't get in my way or try to tell me what to do. I wouldn't have punched out that guy on the Mexico City Metro if he would have just taken no for an answer and got his hands off me.

It's just that when sexual politics creep into the work scene, ugh—I don't even like women that I'm not attracted to kissing and grabbing me like it's part of my job!

WALDO: So after Pablo vented some paranoia about Wagstaff trying to force some kind of official art program on us, we got all checked in, and both did some serious write-ups and doodledowns on all the ideas we were hatching, but it wasn't all work and no play—they realized the dangers of that early on in the space colonization game—we put on our party rags and strutted on through the Bright Sector: Hightown's lavish offduty/leisure/arts/social/shopping section.

I'd never seen anything like it—Pablo told me that Mexico City before the bombings gave it some stiff competition. It was one of the reasons people visited and often decided to move to Hightown, but being there went beyond any of the commercials or publicity holos. The place oozed with electrified goodtimes feelings, no frumpoid workplace this: color, light, music, and smells of shops, restaurants, clubs, galleries of all kinds—touted as all the finest of what the System had to offer. It was where all the hardworking Hightowners—and tourists—came to spend their hard-earned credits and really live a little.

Kind of what the Disney Corp was trying for in their places before they went corpse trying to build Disney Planet.

And it was swarming with people all decked out in gaudy casuals, all desperately trying to have fun; some succeeding to some degree, and a lot looking bored as they strolled, ate, spent, talked, and whatever. Pablo went wild, now and then stopping abruptly to do some vicious caricature in his sketchbook, show it to me, and get us both laughing. There were all kinds there from all over the Mudball and even some born off-planet.

There were also plenty of women. Muchas muchachas, as Pablo put it. We really felt that we were in paradise. We strutted like street studs and went into chase mode.

And it was there that we first got our live and up close looks at Firedrop.

Firedrop! Ay! Qué guapa bellísima! She had one of those slightly overspilling bodies that made her freefall jumpsuit—that hung like a wilted orchid because the Bright Sector is in Hightown's spintank—look like it was melting from the heat of her steaming womanhood. She was a big girl—almost as tall as me—and moved like she was always about to lose her balance but somehow never actually splatted down. Her face blasted a smile that could melt some metals—molten lips, steaming eyes, and glowing skin that looked as if it were just about to start dripping off her skull, but stuck tight anyway.

Both Buck and I wanted her. We thought she looked all right in the media bits we'd seen on her work—but this flesh and flesh, carne a carne, beats out photon simulation anytime.

Lucky for me Buck's shyness froze him awhile. I ándeled into action, grabbed my crayon of the day, opened the sketchbook, and launched into a slasher caricature that I zipped over and flashed her with.

Hey, I caught those dark, flashing eyes. Maybe she was a little overwhelmed by it. Maybe it was too caricatural a caricature and I made that dazzling bridge of teeth burn a few degrees too hot—women can get funny about having their faces deformed—but she noticed me. My name was locked into her memory bank.

Sure, she wouldn't give me her com-

number, but she said she'd look me up in a few weekitos during the Culture Festival.

## FROM A "NEW HIGHTOWN ARTS" INTERVIEW WITH FIREDROP:

(She looks young, in her mid-twenties; the picture quality is that of an obsolate tape.)

FIREDROP: ... it looked awful. I mean, it made *me* look awful ... like a monster, you know, my face was mostly teeth. It was ... powerful, though ... intense ... kinda sexy. Like, the guy had talent.

He was kinda sexy, too.

Kinda scary, too ... like the kinda person you didn't think they'd let into Hightown ... more like a mugger or gangster that they were always catching and making a media spectacle out of deporting back to Earth than some new SCP artists.

I was interested ... you know, I always go for a wild time when I can ... but a girl's got to be careful these days ... especially with artists who look like lowlifes. Bad things can happen to artists who link up with lowlifes.

WAGSTAFF: We usually don't tell artists about format or how they should present ideas to the SCP board. It's a good idea to leave it to their imaginations—and a good way to check out what kind of imaginations they have, if any.

You'd be surprised at the lack of taste and sensibility in the System. Some really hopeless cases get reputations as artists.

Anyway, Cortez and Waldo were a study in contrasts. I could scarcely believe that they had ever worked together. Waldo submitted pristine printouts and cyberdrafted diagrams and read from detailed notes. Cortez literally threw around sketches torn from a sketchbook; including pages of notes in his slashing, spidery handwriting, and talked too fast to be followed as he rambled spontaneously.

Waldo's first tech-art projects were impressive—mostly concerned with large, robotic, interactive sculpture, some for in-colony and others ambitiously proposed for orbital installation. We saw great possibilities for the Festival there.

Cortez's presentation was a scattergun blast of ideas, some workable; like his space hieroglyphics taking cues from ancient art, popular-culture images, and cybersymbols to create a new, strangely accessible visual language; others like his splatterpainting and ideas for environmental pieces that were more terrorism than art.

The board felt unaminously that Waldo showed great promise; and that while Cortez showed unique energy and imagination, in the long run he might not fit into the main thrust of SCP.

We were troubled by the fact that they collaborated on one project for virus programmable graffiti robots; the sort of thing that would appeal more to the criminal element than to the decent citizenry of Hightown.

I worried that Cortez might have been a substance abuser and was being a bad influence on Waldo.

WALDO: Pablo was upset after that meeting. So we went to the Dark Nova, a Bright Sector bar, for a few beers and to listen to Audioverité 9000, a found-noise assemblage band that consisted of a six-foot plus, two-hundred-pound giantess wearing a slashed jumpsuit to which were tied all kinds of things—plastic plumbing fixtures, crumpled insulation sheets, waste-metal bits, and things that couldn't be identified; and her partner, a male dwarf, installed in a playback audio system that threatened to devour him; their music didn't hinder any conversation, only made it necessarily louder.

"I knew this would be the story," he said. "These cabrones only went for the glyphs— a throwaway idea I did to pad my presentation."

"You didn't think they'd go for splatterpainting, did you?" I asked.

He looked at me as if I were the stupidest

thing in the universe. "Look, mira! It's the art that living in space cries out for. It's amazing that nobody ever thought of it before, like in one of those cybersurveys of aesthetic trends."

"It's messy and undignified. Everything they don't want to be."

"And everything that I am. I don't know, maybe all this was a mistake!"

"You think SoCal Beautiful would be easier?"

He laughed. "Those caca merchants? No way. It's just that I want to do splatter-painting—take ancient abstract expressionism to its next logical step into freefall. I'll probably end up doing it anyway. I don't think anything can stop me."

"But they want the space hieroglyphics."

"They'll get 'em. Doing several things at once is biz as usual for me. My family was circus people way back. It's just that sometimes I think I should have went for Project Odysseus instead."

"What? And get your mind sucked dry like Phil Hagen?"

"Yeah, ése, I know. It's dangerous, but then so's living in a space colony, or the L.A. sprawl."

I didn't see much of him until the Festival. He threw himself into his work.

* * *

My roomicito was small, all single-occupant units available to us were, but I was long used to cramped quarters. It was like having my own studio. I locked the door, threw my material around, and went to it. Glyph sketches piled up like crazy, I just unhinged my head and it erupted out of me.

I'd have to raid the can's library now and then for some reference books-on-chip—mostly visual, but some verbal research on Mayan and Egyptian hieroglyphics, Chinese ideograms, pictographs, commercial art, archetypes, comics and manga, advertising, the history of popular imagery et cetera—and get a mediascan to gather and feed me all it could get on Project Odysseus. Then I'd watch as I let it all battle it out in the back of my cabeza: images as metaphors as symbols as codes as messages as masks as thoughts as data as dreams as reality. . . .

FROM II'S "SYSTEM TONIGHT":
(Ex–soap opera star Cleo Karlos rotates her chair to face the holospace behind her.)
CLEO KARLOS: So people really are volunteering to attempt contact with the Sirens?
(A man appears in the holospace: Dr. Lucio Calvino, head of Project Odysseus.)
LUCIO CALVINO: Yes. Surprisingly, we've had more applications for contact-

specialist positions than any other position.

CK: Do these people realize that contact will be dangerous—that what happened to Phil Hagen could happen to them?

LC: The image of Phil Hagen alive, but with his mind seemingly erased from his brain, has loomed large in the popular imagination in the months since the first contact attempt. Still, we've interviewed all applicants at length. They know well what happened to Hagen, and it doesn't bother them—in fact, in a lot of them the idea of that kind of death seems to be more attractive than actually communicating with possibly intelligent alien life-forms.

CK: Gee. I don't understand those people at all.

WALDO: I visited Pablo when I hit a snag in my robosculpture design. His room was thickly coated with sketches. Strange, mad, free-form ideograms based on simplifications of picture symbols used in interlingual signs, but coming alive, dancing off the paper like animated Mayan codices. Images from modern life that seemed to cry out, almost talking.

He put a chip on of the coverage of Phil Hagen's death—it was a popular item in those days—and muttered to me about "visual language."

"... symbols ... they can be stripped, distorted, but your mind keeps seeing messages, or parts of messages. I used to stare at Mayan hieroglyphs for hours; until they seemed to move, squirm, like a magic comic book. Sometimes I wonder if abstract art is possible. How can anything not represent anything as long as an imagination can focus on it...."

I wasn't sure what he was getting at. I'm not even sure he knew what he was getting at. It was more like he was talking to himself, that the monologue would go on even if I wasn't there.

"... I think I'm trying to think like the Sirens...."

Soon he started drawing again. Wasn't even aware of of me. Didn't notice when I got up and left.

The funny thing is, I came up with the space hieroglyphics as a joke—some kind of bizarre satire of commercial art to throw at Wagstaff and the rest of the viejitos if they didn't want the real stuff ... and *that* was what they bought!

I should have figured, with Wagstaff in charge—that zombie grew up thinking Andy Warhol was God and made a career out of creating "cultural icons." An icon maker rather than a iconoclast. No way could we get along.

But, bizarro enough, it got exciting as I got into it. The idea was to cut through Hightown's evolving language barriers—they exist between different kinds of techies as well as nationals and ethnics from the Mudball—but avoid the ugly, moronic clichés like a figure with pants for "man" and one in a skirt for "woman" when both men and women have been wearing pants and dresses for decades and I had to explain to descendants of the Zapotecs at the Museo Rufino Tamayo in Oaxaca which bathroom was which when they were clearly marked with pre-Columbian figurines: one with a penis, the other with breasts and a vagina! Ay, qué loco! So I saturated my mind with picturizations from all cultures and especially current popular comics, cartoons, and advertising to create glyph symbols that danced in the eye and mind until the muy importante synaptic connections were made.

So why's man/woman, male/female gotta be the dressed/pantsed silhouettes or the obsolete Venus/Mars symbols? Why not penis or spermlike forms for the male and vagina/womb/breastlike forms for the female? Or figures based on the Y and X chromosomes? Post-Jungian archetypes!

I even tried to make them readable even if done all locoísimo in dislocated style all jangled around like the wildest works of

last century's graffiti writers. I'd do 'em
wild and twisted ... sometimes splashing
paint. ...

It was almost splatterpainting. Hijolé! I
wanted to do it, so I'd seat some color in
baggies and sneak off to the central freefall
zone, the leisure sections with zero-G sports
facilities, parks, nightclubs, and other easily accessible places where a guy could
spread some paper and do a little experi-
menting in creative applied physics.

WALDO: I was a busy hermit until the
Festival. I was locked into finishing *Roverster One*—my first robosculpture. I'd never
really done anything that complex before.
It nearly drove me mad, but luckily it was
ready to follow me to the installation area
under its own power and steering.

The first thing visible, just after the en-
trance to the Festival area, was a major
work by Wagstaff—a monumental cyber-
painted icon of Phil Hagen at the moment
just after the Sirens left him brain-dead;
that blank look that had already been made
into cheap posters that could be seen everywhere. As usual, Wagstaff had waited until
all the preliminary mythoteching had been
done and moved in, bought a prepackaged
image off the rocks, blown it up to super-
icon size, shown the world its scanline patterns, and messed it up with some sloppy

colorization that most folks don't notice until they look real hard.

I was tempted to sic Roverster on it, but
there were rules here and my creation'd be
able to do some kingkonging and godzilla-
ization soon enough.

Once Roverster was in its pedestal cage
I wandered over to see Pablo's display.
He'd built this modular tinkertoy struc-
ture and attached the hieroglyphs with
glue bullets so they flapped in the air-
conditioner breeze. People in their gaudy,
colorfied offduty clothes trying their best
to have some fun—some even not so dis-
creetly breaking macromeyth crushtabs
under their noses—were drawn in by the
oddball energy and color, but seemed to be
confused by it all.

Pablo was nowhere to be seen.

I cruised around seeing the rest of the
art displays; some good, some bad, some
forgettable. I was about to drift off to grab
a snack and find out where the neat music
was coming from when I nearly ran into
some of Firedrop's sculptures: strange,
fluid forms; sometimes with nonorganic
shapes stuck into them; apparently made
from a fast-solidifying, liquid plastic and
shaped in freefall; also mounted so they
seemed to defy gravity, or what passed for
it in Hightown. Her art was zooming off in
a new direction; these weren't academic

studies of flow mechanics in freefall that anybody could do; they seemed alive and passionate.

There I found Pablo. He was talking to Firedrop. She was dressed to impress, in an outfit with a lot of helium bladders holding it in simulated antigravity and her hair gunked up like it was bubbling over and trying to fly away. He was disheveled and hoodlumish, covered with paint spatters, looking as if he were about to take her hostage. She looked like she wanted to be carried off, and soon.

And a free-lance docudirector was recording the conversation. . . .

## FROM THE DOCUMENTARY *ORBITAL ART BLUES* BY CY YEAWORTH:

(Pablo gently hits one of Firedrop's sculptures. It starts vibrating on the rods it's suspended from.)

CORTEZ: Beautiful. They have no up or down—reminds us that the gravity here is inmitación. Este es la nueva environment realisada. This is what space art should be.

(Firedrop steps closer to him, the floating parts of her dress press against him, obscuring his hands.)

FIREDROP: Yes! Yes! You get it, you understand what I'm trying to do. Is your art freefall-oriented?

(They move closer until their bodies touch.)

C: I want it to be. Muy mucho. I proposed a freefall abstract-expressionist painting project to the SCP board for this Festival, but it was el rejecto grande.

(Firedrop pouts.)

F: I know how that is. I wanted my pieces to be displayed in freefall—you know, like suspended in electromagnetic fields or something like that, but they said it wasn't feasible.

(They run their hands over each other's bodies.)

C: Ay, chiquita! I know, they just don't know when to leave an artist alone.

(Their faces move together. They kiss.)

F: I definitely see what you mean.

(They kiss again. She leans into him. They drop to the ground and roll around, fumbling with each other's clothes. Finally an article of clothing is thrown at the camera . . . )

Yeah, Firedrop and I really hit it off at the Festival. After that interview that made Yeaworth's doc worth seeing, we rushed off to her place—a luxurious condo, her being a successful popularísima artist and all that. After spending the last few weeks in an overstuffed cubbyhole, this was la dolce vita! Ay!

Uh . . . needless to say, we didn't see much of the Festival. We were having a fiesta of our own.

Firedrop—what a locoísima!

She actually revealed to me that her real name was Nancy Feldstein, on that first night that lasted about three days that seemed like one day or one night of hot salsaitas, dripping all over sweet, salty/sweaty flesh.

I was running on nervous energy and adrenaline. She kept putting crushtabs of macromeyth up her nose. . . .

WAGSTAFF: Frankly, I was rather disappointed with Cortez's space hieroglyphics. I figured that such a project would give him a chance to clean up his act and give up all this messy, no-class, badboy stuff. It all looked like variations on themes by a lunatic who was trying to progressively obscure his own symbols by using slapdash techniques derived from 1950's abstract expressionism—the opposite of the future-oriented art that the SCP is trying to promote.

On the other hand, Waldo's Roverster was a tremendous success; the way it stood in its cage folding itself into varying mechanistic anatomies, then broke out to wander the Festival zone providing the attendees with a feeling of participating in the process of art. It was truly wonderful.

Then Firedrop, who was talented but had problems, had to get involved with Cortez ... if only she could have been interested in Waldo instead. . . .

Her snorting macromeyth bothered me. At first I thought it was just something she was doing for the Festival—a boostito to get her through the three weeks of burnout-ization.

She offered me a crushtab, being really polite. I told her about my late parents and ATL.

"ATL," she said. "I'd love to try that. . . . You can't get it anymore. Nobody seems to even remember how to make it."

"There's probably reasons for that," I said. "Like most of the people who knew how to make it are dead—or don't remember ... anything."

"You should try a little macromeyth ... or something," she said while leafing through my sketchbook. "I find that drugs increase my creativity ... help get rid of those nasty old inhibitions. Think of the stuff you'd be able to do. . . ."

"Chica, I ain't never needed any drug to get rid of my inhibitions." I provided an example with my hand. "I got rid of them chingadedas a long time ago. And as far as creativity goes, I'm creative enough as it is. Some people say I'm too creative. Bet Wagstaff would like to buy me a lobotomy."

She laughed. "Wagstaff . . . that tired old faggot gets in everybody's way. He wants to build orbital shrines to the Great God Warhol. . . . If people didn't like my work so much, he'd've sent me back to the Mudball long ago."

"He ain't gonna get in my way. I'm splatterpainting no matter what he says."

"But if the hieroglyphs crash, you're Mudballing it . . . and you can't splatterpaint on Earth."

"I'll figure something out."

"I'll help you."

"Really?"

She snorted another crushtab and said, "Really."

WALDO: *Roverster One* was a hit. The Hightowners loved it. The tourists wanted to take it home. It got more than a fair share of media coverage, and good early reviews.

Then late in the Festival Wagstaff unhooked himself from his husband's muscular arm and walked over to talk to me.

"Mr. Waldo . . . Buck," he said. "Your robosculpture is getting an excellent response. I find it fascinating. It looks like the

SCP will be able to procure funds to sponsor more such projects."

"Great," I said, "I have all kinds of ideas. The next one I want to have . . ."

He reached out and fondled my shoulder. "Tell me later, dear. Raymundo and I have plans."

Then he went off and reattached himself to his man.

I felt excited about being able to do more robosculptures, but at the same time I had a strong yearning to go take a shower.

Eventually, Firedrop and I made our way back to the Festival zone. We'd checked the media and sheets and she and Buck got great reviews: they called him "the tech artist to rearrange Hightown" and said her work "brought new standards to a new art form" but they weren't sure about me from "confusing remnants of an obsolete primitivism" to "a bold departure from the usual SCP clichés."

It made me feel malito, but Firedrop said, "Hey, they're split on Wagstaff's thingie, too. The gal on channel 55 said it was pure kitsch, and this sheet review says Wagstaff has retreated into twentieth-century popism farther than should be possible."

"I guess he may be in trouble, too."

"No way . . . it would take a macrowar to remove him from the SCP."

Then Wagstaff and Raymundo strolled by. I don't think they heard us. They were too wrapped up in each other.

WALDO: Then Pablo and Firedrop caught up with me as Roverster was climbing the Festival's upper scaffolding. They congratulated me on my success, then Firedrop asked if I'd help her argue the case for Pablo's splatterpainting to the SCP board and especially Wagstaff.

"Hey, Pablo and I have been through a lot together. Hell, if it wasn't for him, I'd have never gotten into the SCP. And you belong here, Pablo. The SCP should be sponsoring splatterpainting!"

I said a lot, but then felt a bit uneasy about my success and risking making waves.

Then I remembered what a creep Wagstaff was. . . .

I did a lot of thinking about it.

FIREDROP: Pablo Cortez is one of the greatest artists to come to Hightown. The SCP doesn't realize how lucky they are to have him. So few artists really relate to orbital living the way Pablo does, and his experiments toward splatterpainting are creating something unique that can't be done anywhere but in orbit—which is exactly what the Space Culture Project is supposed to be all about.

This reluctance to encourage this sort of art by the board of the SCP isn't just happening to Pablo. Many other artists—including me—have had innovative space-oriented projects rejected or altered. And a lot of what they're pushing is stuff that could be done on-planet.

This is a major scandal here. We may never end up creating any autonomous space cultures, and the arts will be Mudball-oriented for centuries to come.

No, that'd be awful.

The day after the Festival, Buck called me up.

"Uh, look, Pablo," he said, "I've been thinking about what we talked about the other day."

"Oh yeah. Thanks for agreeing to help Firedrop and me sell splatterpainting. You're a real amigo, man."

"Well, like I said, I've been thinking."

"You're not backing out on us?"

"Well, no. Not really. It's just that, like I said, I've been thinking. You should be careful about how you can do this. If Wagstaff and the others get mad at you, you could get kicked out."

"Hey, it's better than doing things their way, the way they want."

"Like me?"

"Buck, your stuff is great. I like it, and I'm glad that they like it, too; but you're not compromising your principles, your blood, your cojones. You're doing what you want, like a good mad scientist. Right?"

There was a longish pause.

"Yeah. That is right. It's just that I think you should have a backup system or two. Just think up some alternative projects you can pitch, just in case."

"No problema, man. I got these plans doodled out. Murals, like what we did with GMLA, only on a larger scale to be both inside and outside the can."

"Outside?"

"Sí! Can you see it, man? Me working in a space suit and propulsion pack!"

"I can imagine that. I'm glad you've been thinking, too. I'd hate to see you Mud-balled."

"Me too. I gotta say adiós—got these sketches to do."

I hung up and talked to Firedrop later. Mentioned that Buck seemed nervous and worried about confronting the board.

"Your appointment isn't for a couple of days," she said. "Don't worry, he'll be there for us."

WALDO: I was busy with the rough conceptuals of *Roverster Two* when the door buzzed. Of all people, it was Firedrop. She flowed in looking ragged-faced, sleepless, hair unstyled, face unmade-up and somehow jerking around with an artificial energy: a high-power, high-intensity zombie burning hot, hard, and fast.

"Hiya, Waldo guy," she said, flinging herself at my drafting screen. "So . . . this your new robocreature glowing here, mad scientist man? I like it. Cute . . . you really got some stuff going there."

I didn't know what to say. She was acting funny. All hypercharged up but with no direction, just fluttering all over, getting a lot of bruises in the process.

She suddenly threw herself into my lap. Because I was standing up, we both fell into a tangled heap.

"Hey . . . you know that Pablo is a really neat guy and he needs our help. I'd really hate to see him Mudballed. . . . We need more freefall art . . . as much as we need tech art," she said while slowly twining her arms and legs around me.

"I know. I'm going with you and him to his meeting. I'd do anything to help Pablo."

"Oh goody," she said, and laid a killer vampire kiss on me. I was still dizzy when she said, "I'd do anything for Pablo . . . I'd also do anything for . . . with you to keep you on our side. . . ." Her hands slipped under my clothes. She kissed me again.

I don't know why. Maybe my tech training put a few extra logic circuits in my brain. I pushed her away and said, "Look, Firedrop. I'm attracted to you."

"I can see that."

"But Pablo is my friend."

"He's my friend, too. We can all be friends."

"Not this way. I know Pablo fairly well and he wouldn't like this."

"Oh?" she said, snapping away from me. I could almost hear a loud, firm click of something switching in her head—then she popped open her clip-on purse, took out a crushtab, and said, "I got some macromeyth. Ya want some?" while it was en route to her nose.

"Uh, maybe some other time," I said. "I've been working pretty hard—might actually need to rest."

She crushed and snorted and said, "Oh . . . you muddy-foots are so quaint," and bounced out.

I couldn't work and couldn't rest after that scene. Emotions were bubbling over in my guts. So I slid off to Wetware, the nearby techie bar, where a cyberchipjockey shuffled, twisted, crossfaded, multilapped, and distorted selections of the compleat history of recorded music into a suitable sound track for unwinding after a hard session of techwork. After a few drinks I ended up going home with this big, sloppy, highly female-equipped program adjuster woman with a name that consisted mostly of numbers that I don't remember and talked a dialect I could barely make out—but she made me forget about Pablo, Firedrop, Wagstaff, and what a mess this could all mutate into.

WAGSTAFF: It was supposed to be a simple meeting, just Cortez before the board for evaluations of his Festival work and discussion of future projects and funding. What happened looked like some kind of minor insurrection.

Buck Waldo showed up first. Then doc-director Cy Yeaworth. Then a gaggle of mostly young artists and oddball critics. Then Cortez arrived and asked if we could wait awhile.

"This meeting was supposed to be just you and the board," I reminded.

Then a breathless, haggard-looking Firedrop burst in. Things started falling into place. No wonder most of the assembled mob was male!

"Mr. Wagstaff . . . Percy," she said before Cortez could get a word out, "some of us . . . as representatives of Hightown's art community and contributors to the SCP felt that . . . like, we should come here to show our support for Pablo and his experiments in freefall abstract expressionism ... that he calls splatterpainting."

"Don't you think that Mr. Cortez could have done that by himself?"

"Well ... he did propose splatterpainting to the board before the Festival, and it was rejected. Why don't you recall the records and see?"

"There's no need for such action, Firedrop. I remember it all quite well. We found that proposal not nearly as interesting as his other ideas."

"Sure ... and now the space glyphs are treated icy and Pablo's position with us is shaky. One of the best artists up here has an unstable orbit!"

"I wouldn't say that the situation was all that drastic. With all the obvious support this proposal has mustered, the board may be willing to reconsider."

Some of the other board members expressed their agreement.

"But of course," I said, "we'll need to see some examples ... if the arrangements can be made."

Cortez then lifted up a large portfolio, opened it up, and sent several paintings on limp cardboard sailing onto the long table in front of the board members. Everybody in the room scrambled to see them. I was afraid it would turn into some kind of riot.

I must admit the paintings were more interesting than I had expected. They did not look exactly like 1950's abstract expressionism. There was no sense of up or down, no drips, and in some places a unique tridimensional effect where the paint barely stuck to the surface. Cortez twirled them around, showing how they were composed to look "right" from all angles. And there was much talk of "energy," "tension," and "wildness," which they had . . . if one went in for that sort of thing.

Even though I found them messy and undignified, the overwhelming response in the room was positive.

The board moved to support Pablo's splatterpainting project.

It felt like we just had a successful revolución. The Mob, as Wagstaff called us—and even some of the board members—marched off to a nearby art-fart club, called Cabaret Voltron, that was featuring spontaneously generated cybermusic out of Zwart's latest blackbox keyed to interact with conversation and ambient noise. Qué avant-garde! The chic'd out pretenders and hangers-on just loved having their boring small talk musicalized, but for me it plain got irritating after a while—like an obnoxious chamaco mimicking your speech, so you'd end up ordering another drink to help you ignore it. Commercialísimo too!

Despite the hypercharged party atmosphere, I was un poquito bothered. Firedrop was supposed to come over the night before and spend the night with me, then we were gonna go to the meeting together—but she was a no-show.

And to celebrate our triumph, she was talking nonstop about how great an artist I was as if I wasn't there—no eye contact, not a wordito my way, and everything to keep her flesh from accidentally coming into contact with mine.

If that all wasn't stewed caca, she was slithering all over pudgy, old Cy Yeaworth like they were running for couple of the month—giving me a good idea of just where she might have been last night.

After some laughs and chingón talk about el futuro of space art with Buck and the others, and enough drinks to get me to drop the act, I locked my eyes into Firedrop's as she and Yeaworth did things that were impractical with clothes on. They realized that I might be mad after a while, got up as one, and made their four-legged way to the door.

I gulped down the rest of my current drinkicito and went after them, soon snagging Firedrop's free shoulder.

"Where were you last night?" I asked.

"Pablo! You know me, awake for days, then too much sleep," she said, cranking up her smile to max. "Have you met Cy Yea-worth?"

"Yeah, he shot some tape of us at the Festival." He also looked uncomfortable.

"Well, he's decided to make an entire feature-doc on me! It's so exciting. . . . We have just lots to talk about. I'll call you later," she said, gave me a too fast, off-center, dry kiss, and they were gone.

WALDO: I wanted to talk to Pablo about Firedrop, but after a while he was just thinking and staring into space. I knew how he felt about drugs and that he would not appreciate being a mere addition to Firedrop's harem.

Soon he threw his glass at the interactive music machine, which was moisture-proof, and it went into a drippy, liquid-sounding lick as he headed for the door.

Suddenly I was a celebrity. The new hope for space art. Calls for interviews came in until I had to disconnect the phone. And of course la puta grande Firedrop was nowhere to be seen. All I wanted to do was get into my splatterpainting.

The SCP had set up a splatterpainting studio in the freefall core—actually a sort of air-conditioned, airlocked, plastic tent in a disused warehouse area. It was a new world with the old rush of no more gravity combined with the adrenal excitement of a graffiti run and spiced up with the thrill of discovery. I had to learn—and create—ways of flinging paint and moving in freefall. It was like magic, flying and dancing with colorful mutating creatures: the protomorphic beastery of a new mythology. This was a second ritual for outer space. I was a shaman for the new frontier. Madre y Padre would be proud.

And I was doing it all without ATL.

Besides, it took my mind off Firedrop—that and news of the new Odysseus missions being readied to go. I kind of envied those loco volunteers, going through masochistic training that made my parents' neo-Aztec rituals look like fun and games. And I was jealous—more than I was of Yeaworth—of Jean-Claude Chang, for being chosen to be the first of the new "Sirenauts." I'm still jealous. It's crazy.

Maybe my mind got a bit whacked out with those first splatterpaintings. Like weightlessness rearranges your sense of space—up and down depend on how you're looking at things—the pseudo–slow motion of splatterpainting messed with my sense of time. Slow and fast depended on how hard I focused on what, then I'd just plain get caught up in el processo and the hours would slip past me unnoticed—a preview of what the Sirens would do to my perceptions.

Sometimes I'd just let the canvases float around and splat the paint—I kept trying different types and mixtures—at 'em, then look, manipulate, smear, splat some more. . . . It all seemed alive. Like I was communicating with . . . talk about a previewcito!

WALDO: Seemed like Pablo locked himself into the splatterpainting studio and threw away the key. The next time I saw him was on a newschannel flash. . . .

FROM HIGHTOWN NEWSCHANNEL 8 ARCHIVES:
(From a bubble-bagged camera floating in the paint-spattered plastic enclosure with a coverall-wearing, goggled Pablo Cortez.)
NEWSCASTER UNIT: Whatever you think of it, it is new and something that couldn't be done on the Mudball.
(Cortez hits a blob of paint, splattering it over the camera's bubblebag.)
Could this be space art as it was meant to be? Is this human expression reaching for the stars?
(Paint hits a floating, crumpled canvas.
(Cut to Pablo outside the enclosure, with some of his paintings floating around him.)
PABLO CORTEZ: I've always been a

rough-touch painter. Working in freefall has added new dimensions to my work. I make important discoveries every day. It's like exploring unknown planets.

It got so I hated being interrupted. I'd growl in a cross between Aztec warrior and Japanese samurai battle cries and spray splats of paint at the hatch. It kept the tontos away.

Soon I'd just hear the hatch seal pop and would sling paint without even looking and—ay!—it was Firedrop. Got her right in the face. The Martian orange streak was actually an improvement. The macromeyth was getting her all ragged.

"Sorry, babe-ita," I said. "I didn't see it was you. You look like a used burrito."

"I've been working a lot lately ... you know, Cy's been shooting a lot of holotape of me for the doc. Got no time for sleep and other wastes of time."

"So how do I rate a piece of your busy schedule?"

"I saw that news thing on you the other day. It made me miss you. . . ."

"You know where I can be reached. You could also learn to answer my calls."

She tried to look embarrassed. "I know ... I can be a real flake at times ... but you know how it is for an artist here. If you don't keep in the media's mind, you end up splashing down on the Mudball again . . . and . . ." She started fumbling through her purse, sending things floating. "This doc that Cy's doing of me could make me a Systemwide star."

"So you gotta be a puta."

She grabbed a tube full of crushtabs, looked at me, and said, "I know what that word means. You shouldn't call me that . . . I was nice to you."

"Me and a lot of other guys."

She cracked a crushtab. The powder became a white, glowing, exploding nebula that was immediately sucked into a hungry nostril—along with a bead of purple paint. She choked, then sneezed out some sickening glop that hung from her nose by a thin but stubborn umbilical.

"I shouldn't do that in freefall."

"You shouldn't do it at all."

"But . . . I need it. I have so much to do . . . and I don't want to miss anything."

"You've aged years in the last few weeks, becoming a viejita."

"Soon I'll be able to afford treatments to make me look younger . . . and besides, Cy knows these people who can get me these crushtabs, lots of them for a really good price. . . . You need any? I could get you some. Oh, I forgot, you're hung up on that . . . dead parents and all." She grabbed the snot monstrosity and broke the line connecting it with her nose, not noticing that it was stuck to her hand.

I shot some paint at one of my canvases.

"So, like I said," she went on, not noticing my attemptito at ignoring her, "I saw that thing on you on channel 8 . . . you know our work has a lot in common. I thought that my doc should have some scenes of you in it . . . comparing and contrasting your freefall technique to mine. I suggested it to Cy, but he said no, he wants this doc to be purely me. . . ." She laughed, almost. "I think he's jealous . . . are you jealous, Pablo?"

Pretending not to hear, I kept on with my work.

"Dammit, Pablo! I miss you! I've been thinking about you a lot the last few weeks. . . . I could help you, you know!"

"I'm very busy. Leave me alone."

She then noticed the snot clinging to her hand and flicked it onto the plastic, making an instamural à la Firedrop. I left it there for a long time to remind me of her.

"You're a real bastard!" she said as she left.

"Sure am," I shouted at her. "The word 'Chicano' originally meant 'Mexican bastard,' I try not to forget it."

I worked extra hard for a long time. I ended up missing the live coverage of the first new Odysseus contact attempt—had to catch it on a replay from my scan service.

**FROM THE FIRST II/SPACECO PROJECT ODYSSEUS SHOW:**

(Leon Wagner stands before a panoramic viewport on Ithaca Base with Jupiter and the Great Red Spot in the background.)

LEON WAGNER: Greetings, II-ers and Spaceco fans! Tonight, a historic moment that we've all been waiting for, because history just doesn't seem to happen fast enough these days—the first of the new Project Odysseus attempts at communication with the Sirens. Since the heroic death of Phil Hagen just a little over a year ago, Interplanetary Infotainment and Spaceco have joined forces to answer the demands of the System's viewing public for more information about, and if possible, communication with the only life-forms found in the System that did not originate on the Earth. Soon volunteer Sirenaut Jean-Claude Chang will be lowered into the Great Red Spot for his long-awaited contact attempt.

But first, we are privileged to have with us Lucio Calvino, head of Project Odysseus, here to provide some preliminary background.

Hello, Dr. Calvino.

LUCIO CALVINO: Hello, Leon.

LW: Excited about the mission?

LC: You bet. What could be more exciting than scientific research and exploration?

LW: Heh-heh. Couldn't agree with you more, doc, but what do you have to say about all the allegations that Project Odysseus is more show biz than science?

WALDO: Leon should have known all about that. His look and style went from low-budget space cadet to high-rolling game-show host. His questions were now aimed more at gossip than at the wonders of science and discovery. I expected him to sweat out money.

As a kid he was my favorite holohost—I was a sucker for science programs. Now that he hit the big time, I couldn't stand him. That's what success will do to you.

Then I thought about the fat deal I just made with the SCP—a commission for a long series of robosculptures, and for the first time in my life I wouldn't have to beg or steal equipment and materials or even worry about what they will cost.

Would I be able to stand me after a while?

LC: I am not amused by it. This project is, at its core, pure research. It's just dumb luck that public enthusiasm is so great that media coverage has become a profitable commodity. It has been unheard of in the past for such a project to be done without the support and control of a major world government. This could be the first time most of the human race voluntarily sponsored such an enterprise.

LW: And you can count me as one of its biggest fans.

LC: As well as an employee?

LW: Heh-heh. I'm supposed to ask the questions here, doc. Speaking of which, what about those that raise the question of the morality of a scientific endeavor that sends people on what are essentially suicide missions?

LC: Believe me, Leon, no one who works on this project hasn't spent some long hours thinking about that question. Yes, there is a chance that every Sirenaut may die a death similar to that of Phil Hagen—it's something they are reminded of many, many times before the final contracts are signed. Spaceco's legal department has been very careful about this. But this is not very different from any other kind of dangerous work such as military microwar specialties, heavy industry of many kinds, and, yes, this very dangerous thing called space exploration.

Also, some of us have theorized that Phil Hagen's death may have been a fluke. He had sustained no physical damage, all vital signs were just as if he were still alive. His brain death was like a recording tape or a datachip being blanked. The first zapware death, as the media has called it. It may have been something that had more to do with Hagen than the Sirens.

It may be that Jean-Claude Chang and all his fellow Sirenauts will survive to give countless postmission interviews.

LW: But just in case, the Odysseus dirigi-scaphes are equipped with the System's most advanced telemetry software so that information will be gathered even if the Sirenauts die.

LC: Yes, but the Sirenauts are not really involved in most of the information gathering. They are there more to test the effect of the Sirens on the human nervous system.

LW: Or, to phrase it differently, to see if zapware death will occur.

LC: A necessary part of the research.

LW: But some critics have said that that is the reason most of the System is tuning in to watch tonight's mission.

LC: I'd prefer to think that most people aren't so morbid.

I didn't agree with Calvino about the nobility of the human race. Most of them could get muchísimo morbid if you asked me. Then, that wouldn't be the last time he and I had our differences.

The appeal of Project Odysseus to most

eager viewers was the same as that of the Roman arena, the bullfight, and the Aztec sacrifice: sangre, blood; muerte, death. Just plug into any kind of network, run through the entertainment channels, and there it is, real and simulated, in movies and micro-wars; pain and death. Yesterday's terrorist is the hero of tomorrow's miniseries.

As mi padre was always saying, "All cultures have some acceptable form of human sacrifice. And if you really want to cause trouble, try taking it away."

It's the twenty-first century, and the System is going Aztec.

LW: Well, we'll be seeing that mission soon, but first, this clip of a talk I had with Sirenaut Jean-Claude Chang.

(Cut to a leisure section of Ithaca Base. Jean-Claude Chang lounges in a large, baggy chair.)

LW: (offscreen): I understand that your approach to the contact attempt is rather unique?

J-CC: Aren't we all unique?

LW: So, what are the specifics of your approach?

J-CC: I am a student of Zen. I have practiced meditation for twelve years. The ability to clear my mind of everyday modes of consciousness, I believe, will keep my mind from overloading during zapware contact with the Sirens.

LW: Yet there isn't much as far as concrete scientific evidence for your approach.

J-CC: No, so far this part of the project is rather informal, but in this century many of us have learned that we must believe in more than what the senses can reveal. I have kept up a strict routine of daily meditation along with the standard Sirenaut training. I've trained my mind—my soul, if you will—as well as my body. I believe I will survive.

WAGSTAFF: Jean-Claude was such a handsome young man. Beautiful, really. Long, sandy brown hair. Blue eyes that looked like frozen gases. And the Chinese cast to his features made him all the more elegant. A clean-shaven, blond Christ. A face and figure destined to be art.

(Cut back to Calvino and Wagner live from the Ithaca observation deck.)

LW: We've received word from Mission Control that Jean-Claude Chang's dirigiscaphe has entered the Great Red Spot. We'll switch to a live feed. . . .

(Cut to the dirigiscaphe's onboard camera, showing a close-up of Jean-Claude Chang's face peeking from inside his exoskeleton.)

MISSION CONTROL (offscreen): Jean-Claude, has the ship stabilized?

J-CC: Yes. Descent has ceased. Readings show that many Sirens are near. I am going to start meditation now.

(Chang closes his eyes, starts taking slow, deep breaths while humming a mantra. All expression leaves his face.)

WAGSTAFF: At that moment, just before contact, while he was meditating, his face took on such a look of pure beatitude. He became perfection.

MC: Zapware activity strong. Zapware strikes on vehicle.

(Chang starts to smile as tiny lightning bolts slide over his face. His eyes open. He laughs.)

Ay! I started to laugh, too. So hard it hurt. At the time it all seemed hilariousísimo.

(Chang laughs harder, then stops. His face is frozen in the position of laughter.)

WAGSTAFF: It was the complete opposite of his previous beatific face. The other side of the coin. I was suddenly thinking in terms of a double icon, showing both faces.

WALDO: It made me sick, literally. I ran to my toilet and puked my guts out. Then I sat and shivered for the longest time. I shut off the holo, but I couldn't get that feeling of knowing that Jean-Claude Chang was dead out of my mind. I kept seeing his face. . . . I tried to work, but couldn't, just paced for hours—then sat down, shifting around nervously. Finally, somehow— probably pure exhaustion—I fell asleep.

And I had a nightmare: I was working on an exoskeletal robosculpture, making all kinds of fine adjustments so it would fit me perfectly, then I got into it, was ready to activate, when all kinds of snaky little light- ning bolts began to lick me all over; it felt like my body was dissolving. Then the exo- skeleton/robosculpture opened up and spat my body out—but *I* was still inside the ma- chine, looking at my own corpse through cybereyes. I tried to move the sculpture's arms and legs, but they refused to obey me. The machine just walked away, dragging me as a prisoner along inside it. It started punching holes through Hightown's outer walls, each one larger, until finally, it/I fell through one, out into space—and there was Jupiter, clouds boiling, the Great Red Spot engulfing me like a monstrous, hungry mouth, and then it *was* a mouth, with teeth the size of icebergs and a tongue like a great, warty megawhale. It chewed me—the exoskeleton/robosculpture/me. More lightning: this time planet-strangling serpents instead of baby snakes swam through oceans of acidic saliva that dissolved me in a boiling electric firestorm. Then I—what there was left of me—expanded. I was as big as Jupiter. Then I was Jupiter, the big planet, the Sirens, the clouds, the lightning, the radiation, and radio waves flashing in and out of the magnetosphere like a cosmic beacon. I was swirling, crackling energy, swirling faster, getting stronger until I exploded—destroying the universe—creating the universe—waking up, shaking, soaked in ice-cold sweat.

I picked up the phone, punched up the local Spaceco officito, asked for the info about volunteering for Odysseus—even had them transmit me hard copies.

I don't know why I did it. I guess I was just curious. At the time I had no intention of volunteering. Nada. Not even un poquito. I just couldn't help myself. Yo soy loco.

WALDO: It seemed that all anyone could talk about for weeks was Jean-Claude Chang. Even news of the capture of Hightown's major drug gang was preempted by talk of him. Not as much him—nobody really knew much about him, or even cared, minidocs on his life were blipped over—but his death, that strange, quiet, laughing death. Everywhere I went, that chip seemed to be playing, end-lessly, on every screen. And everybody—except for maybe me and a few other lost souls—loved it.

Comments came from everywhere, filled the air, and ended up rattling around in my head:

"I never knew death could be like that."

"It's just that almost everybody in the System looked into his eyes and saw him go. It changed everything."

"We saw death up close. Now we really know what it is to be alive."

"Do you think the Sirens did it on purpose?"

"Maybe we're not worthy of contacting them."

"I think we should nuke that gasbag and kill every one of those microbastards!"

"Makes one wonder: what's everything all about anyway?"

I got sick of it all fast—but everybody else couldn't get enough of it.

Even Pablo—who's usually the noncon-formist's nonconformist—was into Zapware Death Mania. But, as usual, he was coming at it from a different angle than the rest of humanity:

"Ay! If Picasso only knew what he started when he remembered what Western civili-zation forgot when it learned perspective, but then a lot of us never forgot in the first place, and still remember *after* we've learned perspective. And with the Sirens, the relationship between the conceptual and the perceptual is being rethought again.

"It's all those signs and symbols that everybody hangs their cabezas on. They get hooked too hard there, confusing style with substance, el mapa with la tierra. Like what that good ol' gal Maria was always saying about televoodoo—smash someone's symbols and their hearts and minds shatter away," he said, not really caring if anyone was hearing.

"Maybe that's what gets to me about it," I said as he splattered mustard and Tabasco sauce in a creative pattern on his hamburger. "The symbols crack, death opens its eyes and laughs from the home of electric storm germs ... it's like the universe turned upside down."

"Yeah, ain't it great," he said, then devoured his latest creation.

I let my pizza stick cool and droop. It was no use talking to him. He was too deep into his own explorations.

Later, I tried to throw myself into my work like Pablo, but I had a hard time concentrating. It all kept slipping away. Soft, furry, headless, tailless dinosaurs that moved in slow motion so the kiddies could play on them kept growing thorny scales,

fangs, and claws. My creations were fran-
kensteining on me.

And if all that wasn't enough, Firedrop
had to die and really turn Hightown upside
down.

I was doing my usual splatting away
when the splatterstudio bubble began to
shake like a big drum. Ay, ay, ay! I thought,
I've done it now, splattered my mind as well
as the paint— "This time you have gone too
far!"—so all the Aztec heavens came rain-
ing down in jagged pieces like ceremonial
knives. Had I televoodoo'd myself? Was this
the first zapware death sans Sirens?

No.

It was Buck, eyes about to pop out of
those thick glasses, pounding on the walls
around the door seal like he'd gone berserk.

For un momento I figured that maybe it'd
be a good idea to keep the seal locked and
hope he'd go away; but upon a few seconds
of eye contact, he calmed down, said something in a way that would have been meaningful if I could read lips, so I figured I'd
risk letting him in just to find out what he
had to say.

"Better brace yourself," he said, hanging
on to the door for dear life, looking as if he
were about to be freefall sick.

I grabbed my knees and hovered.

"It's Firedrop," he said, almost in tears. "She's dead. Macromeyth overdose."

I was glad my face was freefall-bloated. Besides, I hadn't taken off my goggles.

"It happened this morning—or last night. It's all over the can cables. We could go plug in somewhere—"

"No," I said, grabbing my paint stick. "I think I better stay here . . . and work. . . ."

"Okay," he said, leaving. "Sorry if it upset you. I knew you liked her. Thought you'd wanna know."

Somehow beads of tears were floating inside my goggles.

WAGSTAFF: It was a real shame. Firedrop was such a talented young person, if rather erratic. Never quite achieved her full potential, if you ask me.

And there was no reason. These days we have remarkable educational programs on recreational drug use in all the schools. To be frank, she simply *had* to know better.

Her passing did cost the SCP one of its most popular and best-selling artists. Though it was some consolation that all her existing work went up in price.

Then there was Cy Yeaworth's doc about her, completed just in time to cash in on her demise. After her corpse was found in his condo. And his taping his epilogue, literally over her dead body, was the very height of tastelessness.

FROM *FIREDROP: THE RISE AND FALL OF A FREEFALL ARTIST*, A DOCUMENTARY BY CY YEAWORTH:

(The picture quality is suddenly worse—shot with a home holocam that Yeaworth set up himself just after discovering Firedrop's body. It focuses on the body, not very well, and Yeaworth walks on camera, squatting over the corpse, which is sprawled on his bathroom floor, next to the toilet.)

YEAWORTH: Wow. Uh, I guess I have me a real killer—damn, wish I hadn't used that word—well, a sensational ending for this doc.

(He sniffs. Wipes a tear.)

God. I wish it wasn't this way. I probably don't have to tell you that Firedrop and I were quite an item—we were seen together all over Hightown. The business relationship we had developed into a real romance . . . the best I ever had. I'm gonna miss this woman—this artist.

(He breaks down, cries a little.)

Better cut it here.

I couldn't believe that ending! Of all the gall! I knew that pendejo Yeaworth was a slime capsule, but this was el último. . . .

To see her there—dead—really got to me. I couldn't watch that final scene. The rest of the doc just about killed me, but that ending . . .

Suddenly I was acting like Buck after Jean-Claude Chang's zapware death, only worse.

I didn't want to talk to anyone about it. I sealed myself into the splatterstudio and worked like I was possessed.

It all got more and more violent. I threw away the paint stick and began slopping the stuff right out of the cans—I wanted super-splatterísimos! Then I mixed it with thinned media and retardants so it would flow freer and not dry so fast or eventually at all. Then I began tearing up the canvases, tying them in knots, then threw them into the studio and set up fans to blow them in wild currents through the studio. Now and then I'd punch a hole in those flimsy plastic walls and swirling stuff'd spill over into the free-fall warehouse, which I knew would get me in trouble, but I was so worked up like I had tres cojones and could outscream and outintimidate anyone.

Some wild días there.

WALDO: So Pablo calls me one day demanding that I meet him at the splatterstudio. "Wear old clothes or a throwaway wrapper," he warned.

When I got there, it looked like the inside of a polluted washing machine—paint shloshed around like a liquid storm. Through what wasn't splashed on the walls I could barely make out Pablo, who was flailing around like he was either drowning in a maelstrom or fighting for his life with invisible demons. I couldn't get his attention, which was okay, because even with the wrapper I didn't really want to go in there.

Then a section of the wall gave way right in my face, vomiting paint, canvas, and a wild Pablo who said, "Hijolé! I can hardly wait to spring this on the board!"

WAGSTAFF: Suddenly Cortez was badgering us to see what he was up to. He was really excited, but then he always was such an excitable young man. He did keep on, relentlessly, so I made space in everybody's schedule for an informal meeting at his splatterpainting studio.

It looked like a disaster area—a paint warehouse ravaged by bomb-throwing maniacs. And Cortez was also covered in splattered paint—layers of it. It looked as if he were rolling in his canvases, or at least getting too close to them. He insisted on flinging them around in freefall and they were still wet, showering the entire board with a rain of paint.

All the while he babbled the way he does;

talking a little too fast to be properly understood and littering his speech with Spanish words and Spanishisms.

I wasn't the least bit amused. Neither was anyone else on the board; even those members who had originally supported the splatterpainting project.

The disapproval was obvious as we all examined the paint that had ruined our expensive suits.

I must admit, it gave me quite a bit of satisfaction.

Cortez was oblivious to what was happening. He just floated with a ludicrous grin on his paint-covered face.

I told him we'd discuss it with him later.

I went back to my room, wishing there were some way I could turn off the chingada gravity there, still wearing all that paint—that was still wet and getting all over everything—my face starting to hurt from that grin. An explosive happinessísimo roared through my bloodstream—los throbthrobthrobos blotting out the entire universe. I put on some of Vacuum Noise's subsonic music, then flicked on my holoscreen, didn't really pay attention, let the nadaladeda breeze by until this incredible commercial came on. . . .

* * *

II/SPACECO PROJECT ODYSSEUS COMMERCIAL:

(Open on space, zoom in to Jupiter, then the Great Red Spot fills the screen. Dissolve to a dirigiscaphe entering the Jovian atmosphere. Dissolve to close-ups of Phil Hagen, then Jean-Claude Chang, then to Leon Wagner on an elaborate studio set with a view of Jupiter in the background.)

LEON WAGNER: Big news, Odysseus fans! Interplanetary Infotainment and Spaceco—thanks to the enthusiastic support of you, the System's viewing public—have made a deal that will allow us to bring you a new Project Odysseus Siren contact mission every week as a regular Systemwide network show. Interest in science has reached new heights!

(Cut to a still of an athletic-looking, auburn-haired, freckle-faced young woman.)

LW (offscreen): So check your local listings to see your time next Monday night when II and Spaceco will bring you this young woman, Sophie Wright, as she faces the Sirens.

(The still of Wright comes to life.)

SOPHIE WRIGHT: I think I'll survive. I'm using the hardheaded, scientific approach, influenced by old NASA psychological training.

(Cut back to Wagner.)

LW: Well, we all hope you survive, Sophie! See you Monday!

(Wagner's image tilts and shoots off into the starscape.)

. . . and with the happinessísimo and los throbthrobthrobos multiplied a zillion times. It seemed that all was right with the universe.

I was wallowing in it for a gordo eternity. Then the phone rang.

It took me a few rings to sort it out from the intoxicating chaos. I got my nalgas up and clicked on the phone. Wagstaff's zombified face appeared on the screen.

He was hilarious. I laughed.

"I'm glad you're in such good spirits, Mr. Cortez," he said, looking like un poquito laughito would crack and crumble him like a late-night-show vampire.

"Okay, jefe," I said. "Gimme your baddesto. I'm feeling too good to be slowed. So arriba! Ándele!"

After a look of agonized constipation, he said, "The board had a meeting after your—uh—presentation. And it was unanimously decided that nothing you've created in the splatterpainting project is usable for SCP purposes. We also question your competency and suitability for working with us."

I found myself laughitoing again. Couldn't help it.

"The space hieroglyphics you started out with were at least interesting, but everything you've done since has become more and more unacceptable. Too messy. Dripping all over the place . . ."

"Look, Señor Maricón! All I did was what you asked me to—what the SCP was set up for in the primero place!—come into this nuevo environment and create a nuevo art for it. It developed into splatterpainting, not the uptight, contrived burgués kitsch you lust after," I said, finding myself witty.

"You should really be more cooperative," he said, with his tight, crisp facade, more acrylic than flesh, about to chip.

"Last time I heard that I was shot," I said, going into a rant. "What you want isn't art. It's municipal garbage, state-sponsored toromierda, committee-conceived caca!"

Ay! His face twitched. More than once. I hit an en vivo nerve, struck pain, scored a few points.

Then he puckered up his face and spat out, "I'm afraid we can't waste money on you any longer. We'll have to send you back to Earth!"

"No! You don't understand me and I'm human; from your world! If you can't deal with me, how do you expect to face the rest of the universe? What are you doing out here anyway?"

"Settle your personal affairs. We'll be contacting you to work out the details of your departure later," he said, then the screen flicked to visual white noise.

I still don't know why, but I laughed more—el vato es loco—did a teleroulette spin that kept my eyes occupied as I kept the chuckle going.

Then I saw good ol' Cy Yeaworth's bloated face, and alto'd it a sec.

FROM HIGHTOWN NEWSCHANNEL 8 ARCHIVES:

(Old publicity still of Cy Yeaworth.)

NEWSCASTER UNIT: Well-known art-doc-maker Cy Yeaworth was found dead in a freefall cargo section today. Hightown Security is not disclosing details at this time, except that they feel this death has to do with connections Yeaworth had with parties illegally distributing drugs in Hightown.

I laughed harder. For a while I actually believed in televoodoo more than that spookada Maria Davis. I wished I had given that homely muchacha more than that one sloppy French kiss. I felt—if you pardon el cliché grande—inspired.

It was then that I called Hightown's Spaceco office to volunteer for Project Odysseus.

WAGSTAFF: I was sure he had gone mad—the way he kept laughing hysterically. I wasn't the least bit surprised that he volunteered for Odysseus.

I was rather looking forward to making an icon of him. Despite his peculiarities, he was pleasant to look at.

WALDO: Things were finally in control with the robosculptures again. Then this nukehead about Pablo hit me. I rushed off, tried to find him. He wasn't home. Finally, I caught up with him at what had just become the ruins of the splatterstudio.

"I wandered through las ruinas all over Mesoamerica," he said, looking naked with the paint scrubbed off him. "Now I got some of my very own—too bad they ain't gonna last too long."

"I heard the bad news," I said. "Is there anything I could do? I do have some clout with the board—I could talk to them."

"Naw," he said, continuing with his violent dismantling. "It's too late for that. Besides, I got this contract with Spaceco and a date with the Sirens."

"They accepted you already?"

"Gotta take some testitos, and process some legal mumbo jumbo, but they want as many of us as possible—expect the show to last for years!"

"You could die."

"Don't be too sure, Buck. A loco like me don't get finished so easy. Besides, you know me, ése, I got itchy feet, need to wear down my zapatos—and SCP and me don't get along so great. You know me and rules."

"I don't seem to have any trouble here."

"But you ain't me. Maybe this can just isn't big enough for the both of us. You gotta keep it up, Buck. Knock 'em muerto, become a chingón. Make sure the SCP actually lives up to some of its pretensions."

"Yeah, I guess a mad scientist's gotta do what a mad scientist's gotta do."

"You bet, ése! And another thing . . ."

"What?"

"Try to make some graffiti bugs and turn 'em loose around here. These walls could use some placas."

And I did it. I'm one of the SCP's greatest success stories. My robosculptures and monsters are commissioned all over the System. I even made a big deal with the Rouse Media Corp to work on some of their monster movies. I'm not as famous or influential as Pablo, but I can't really complain.

After all, I can afford to sneak away and work on secret projects that just make me feel good . . . like graffiti bugs and other things that go buzz in the bright.

I was actually looking forward to leaving Hightown. It was fun while it lasted, but if you don't watch, space-colony life really does become canned life—might as well be locked into some suburbito. That's why I like to keep on moving.

And there was this big, beautifulísimo Spaceco transport, the *Mothra*, waiting to take me to the gate to whatever. . . .

However, seeing Sophie's Wright's almost live zapware death made me feel a bit uneasy.

# = 4 =
## Mothra

(Willa is getting excited. She knows this is
the part when she came in. And there you
are, mi bonita, popping up in the paint
again . . . or did my hand put you there?
Qué guapa. Of course, the camera snakes in
for a close-up.

What was that question Anna just asked?
Oh yeah.)

No, I did not enjoy all those months on
the *Mothra* on the way to Ithaca Base. It
was an HL79, designed by one of Spaceco's
military subsidiaries for some mad plan
that was happily never put into action in
these days of microwars and cyberterror-
ism. It had the obligatory wheel to simulate
one-G, which is standard equipment on all
interplanetary vehicles, but also a segunda
wheel that spun faster to simulate *two*-G!

Somebody figured that it'd be a great way
to train spacrines to be double-muscled in-
vader grunts out of some twentieth-century

sci-fi. Somebody else thought it'd be great to train athletes. And some other mofo figured that since us Sirenauts would have to deal with Jovian ultragravity, they'd be great for training *us*!

To make matters worse, I was put in the clutches of two doctors who seemed to think that the best way to prepare us for zapwarization was to try to destroy us in their own sweet ways. A pair of real amorcitos. Dr. Muhammud Ali Gorog, space shrink . . .

## DR. MUHAMMUD ALI GOROG'S PRELIMINARY PSYCHOLOGICAL EVALUATION OF PABLO CORTEZ:

The subject is an artistic type with the usual personality features combined with a fierce individualism bordering on the pathological, all possibly the result of his having been raised a member of an ethnic group and living between subcultures; an example of this in sociology is called the marginal man, who, in his bicultural situation, is unable to fuse with the mainstream of society or carry on the traditional culture of his minority group, withdraws from social norms, and engages in a lifelong, frustrated rebellion without focus.

Cooperation and subordination may be a problem, but his talent for pattern recognition and ability to adapt to new environments and understand new ideas—he understands science more than most artistic types—may be helpful in surviving a Siren experience. Also, verbal and visual self-expression would be helpful, if indeed he does survive.

Though he calls himself an "all-purpose heathen," his conversation often is littered with Aztec references, the result of an early neo-Aztec upbringing by parents who died too soon. This all contributes to an identity crisis that he deals with through an idomatic egomania.

All of the above, combined with the fact of his being entertaining, make the subject prime Sirenaut material.

... and mission doctor/physical training manager Magda Koscina ...

## DR. MAGDA KOSCINA'S PRELIMINARY PHYSIOLOGICAL EVALUATION OF PABLO CORTEZ:

The subject is in relatively good health for a young man in his late twenties. No serious medical problems, but lack of discipline in life-style and exercise have taken their toll.

Also, prolonged work in freefall environments has caused the beginning of Freefall Adjustment Syndrome—which will have to be countered with extra exercise if he's to survive Jovian gravity, even with an exo-skeleton.

Though enthusiastic about Project Odysseus, he shows signs of uncooperativeness in physical training sessions. Extra pressure will be necessary. If he can be made to go through the exercise program, he will do fine.

She was this gigantic musclebound old broad of Eastern European extraction. He was a small, thin-boned, dried-up Arab of some sort. I didn't get along with either of them.

The only thing that made vida worthwhile on that trip was meeting Willa.

DR. MUHAMMUD ALI GOROG'S PRELIMINARY PSYCHOLOGICAL EVALUATION OF WILLA SHEMBE:

The subject is shy and withdrawn and shows the typical dissociative socialization of someone whose formative years were spent in a country undergoing an upheaval like that of Zululand in the last two decades. She was also the subject of research into extrasensory perception conducted by the newly formed University of Soweto. All experiments were inconclusive and skewed by the indigenous beliefs of the researchers, and left the subject with a severe adolescent trauma.

Lack of basic social skills may interfere with training, but apparent ability and obsession with indirect insights into the thoughts of others may prove useful in hypothetical communication with the Sirens.

## DR. MAGDA KOSCINA'S PRELIMINARY PHYSIOLOGICAL EVALUATION OF WILLA SHEMBE:

The subject is underweight with lack of muscle tone due to malnutrition and lack of exercise in formative years. Metabolic slowdown that normally occurs at her age could result in weight gain and many physical problems. If it weren't for the lack of any specific malady, I would suggest disqualifying her from the program.

Training will have to be extra severe on this subject. Diet and exercise must be radically altered if she will make it as a Sirenaut.

Ay! Qué Willa! That beautiful, perfect Zulu face, those impossibly intense eyes— beauty that puts the cold, marble-white classicism of dead and buried ancient Greece to shame, causing arrogant statues to crack and crumble to dust—making you see how right the barbarians were in knocking their heads off. A presence that is soft, yet extremely powerful, like the fearfully soft swishing of a skirt that reveals the presence of an umkhovu—a Zulu zombie—lurking about like a bad memory of apartheid.

I first noticed her in one of those early, bore-arama orientation sessions back in Hightown, weeks before *Mothra* was ready for the voyage. I had never seen the likes of this chica—the way that dark, almost purple skin shined! The heart-melting expression of her face. My glands forced my brain into pursuit mode. I had to have her.

I didn't see her again until the final boarding of *Mothra* several long weekones later. By then my sketchbook—SCP had taken away my studio space—was full of wild, slashing renderings of Willa.

Since lack of work space forced me back to nonliquid media—kiddies' crayons, my usual choice within those límites—and cut me off from freefall, my work regained its figurative nature; though now my approach was freer, faster, more deliciously distorted.

I had an el maestro plan about how I was going to set things up so I could todo nonchalante show her my sketchbook, but the schedule was strangle tight for the first several weeks—all kinds of orientation sessions on how to live and behave in an interplanetary spacecraft in tedious detail and designed as if we were all supposed to be idiotas grandes. No time for any socializing with fellow Sirenauts other than shared subvocal complaints and occasional meaningful eye contact.

And, ay! I contacted those space black/bright eyes of Willa's a few times. . . .

But I didn't get into any real contact with her until this awful exercise session in the double-G wheel. . . .

INCIDENT REPORT BY DR. MAGDA KOSCINA:

Willa Shembe was slow in keeping up with the group workout. I felt that she needed to be made to work harder in her individual session. She was trying, but not hard enough to be effective. I raised my voice.

Suddenly Pablo Cortez came running as fast as he could in double-G. Coming to her rescue, so to speak.

A connection has been established between these two. I believe it could be manipulated to solve Cortez's insubordination problem as well as encourage Shembe to exercise.

I will discuss this with Dr. Gorog.

Once we were back in single-G, Willa and I stuck together. Everybody was getting into the training routine, so the pendejos started giving us bits of slack time between exercise sessions, equipment study, and mission simulation. We took to the slack like sharks to an underwater charnel house. Most of the socializing was intense but superficial, probably because watching the Project Odysseus show every week, we realized that there wasn't much of a chance of survival—for the others, that is—and nobody wanted to get too close to any potential corpses.

But, ay! That starts triggering locoization fast, you start itching for a friend, a buddy.

And now the ice was going meltdown between Willa and me. I was hoping I'd slide into a little more than the usual buddy business.

We ate together. Space burritos. Yucko.

"I really hate these chingadedas," I told her. "Sure, they're practical in some stupid way with gummed tortillas that glue themselves shut and formulated unimashed filler that couldn't drip if it tried."

"Mine are bad, too," she said. "The diet they have me on."

I chomped mine. "My diet ain't so bad, just un poquito short on spices. Needs some picanteing up. What I wouldn't give for a big, greasy, homemade taco, dripping with red-hot salsaita. Even in freefall! I'd smear it on me, and the walls. There ain't no kind of food that can't be wrapped in a tortilla! It's a chance to be creative! The burrito can be an art form! People are always blowing it, nuking their cultures."

"Eating," she said. "I do not like it much."

She didn't seem too happy, so I drew a quick caricature of her on the tabletop with the bland stuff that Spaceco had the nerve to call taco sauce.

She smiled. Not much on talking, my Willa, but what she can say with a smile . . .

Soon I was showing her my sketchbook. I could tell she was blushing by the way she fanned herself.

Words, in tiny bits and pieces, came from her. She told me about the experiments for the U of Soweto's department of parapsychology, her telepathic abilities, shyness, and insatiable curiosity.

I even started believing she could read minds when she moved away just before I tried to slip my arm around her.

She didn't run away, though.

After a while she was leaning against me as I doodled in my sketchbook, and she wrote in that diary that the U of S parapsych researchers got her into the habit of keeping back in her early years.

FROM WILLA SHEMBE'S DIARY:

I have made a friend here. Pablo Cortez, an artist from Los Angeles. I cried while Dr. Koscina yelled at me. He yelled at her.

I like Pablo, but he is scary. His head is full of images. Some sex images, too. Him and me.

Being near him makes me feel good, but he is strange, loud, and scary. It does make this routine workable.

## PROGRESS REPORT BY DR. MUHAMMUD ALI GOROG:

The relationship between Cortez and Shembe is to be encouraged. As a result of it, both have begun working harder at their training. Shembe's exercise and diet programs are now working smoothly. Cortez has become more cooperative overall.

After a while I—naturally, macho that I am—wanted sex. A couple of months of monking it while largely disoriented was okay, but you can even get used to things like Sirenaut training after a while; things seem almost normalcito, even in the double-G wheel, doing group exercises in what looks like slow motion and feels like moving through the bottom of a Jell-O ocean with all your muscles running at half power and Koscina barking to keep us moving in time with Amy Woolrich's Systemic hit "Ecstasy Blues." To make it all worse, sweat in double-G runs down bodies and hits the floor twice as fast, and makes a chico think about doing other kinds of ex-

ercises as some female bodies in soaking
exersuits move not quite within grabbing
distance!

Willa seemed to like me a lot, but getting
her to let me touch her was mucho
rougho. . . .

WILLA: Pablo wants sex. I see it in his
mind images. I am the partner he wants.

I have tried to tell him what physical contact does to someone with my abilities. The
feeling, emotions are so intense. Too intense. Hurt.

He has a hard time realizing this.

I was getting so I couldn't stand it. Willa
kept giving me this sci-fi about sex hurting
a telepath like her. I wondered if maybe she
just didn't like me all that much.

So who could blame me when this sultry
Sirenautess from Australia with exotic part-
abo looks and muscular body swelling like
a female should, starts giving me the eye bit
in double-G that after a few days of hot
looks I don't start talking to her instead of
Willa—typical small talk about how that
Sirenaut last week who tried the militarist/
athletic approach . . . funny, with one every
week it was getting hard to remember their
names—died with such a strained grimace
on his face and it was starting to look as if
no one would be able to survive contact,

that we should live for el momento and go for those impulsitos? Soon we were in my cubicoid impulsing each other the way we both needed so bad.

I figured it was the beginning of a beautiful friendship.

Later on, when we were cooled off, redressed, and ready for a scene shift, we opened the door and there in the hall, dark eyes wide, thin body trembling like it was going to fall apart, was Willa.

WILLA: I could feel what they did. Emotional attachment with him was getting too strong. It made me sick.

She became ashamed and went away. He played hard, but was ashamed inside.

"Look," he said, "I got my needs."

Talking was hard. Harder than writing. Words hard. Images better.

"Pablo," I said. "I love you."

"You certainly are making it difficult."

I cried. "You can have me."

I felt like I was in one of the goddess Chalchuitlicue's—storm goddess; wife of Tlaloc, the rain god; mistress of uncontrolled emotions and young, picante love/lust—passion whirlpools. It didn't seem real. She looked like she was gonna die.

She collapsed against me. It felt like I was holding up a sack of wet rags.

"It will hurt me," she said. "But I can't let that ... happen again."

"Look, mi vida," I finally said. "Ms. Aboid left me worn out. And you don't look quite like you're in the best shape either. Why don't we ... just relax awhile?"

So we went into the cubicoid, got on the bed. She collapsed even more, yet kept trying to cling to me. I turned on the two-D monitor, didn't really care what to—we just needed to warm the room.

After a while I remembered it was time for the Odysseus show. . . .

WILLA: Pablo turned on the monitor. I couldn't watch the show. My mind. It all came back. In little flashes:

The cool, clean buildings of the parapsychology lab.

Wires stuck on to my shaved head. Do this, do that. Damn you, girl, this is all very important! Tell us what you sense.

That scary doctor with his broad, dark face and deep, roaring voice. Why can't you do what we ask? Pay attention, girl! I'm sorry. Don't cry. It is so important that we get results, dear. There, there. Did I ever tell you that you are very pretty?

His hands on my face. My lips. My neck. My leg. My body.

With this new equipment we can let your hair grow.

Let's have lunch together, Willa.

You are really quite pretty the way your hair has grown back.

He locks the door one day, that day.

Just relax, Willa. Today we take things easy. Isn't it hot in here? Let me help you unbutton that. There, you should feel much better now. You really are a pretty girl. You are becoming a beautiful young woman.

His lips, hands. On me, under my clothes. Tearing. I fall out of my chair.

You clumsy little fool! Don't fight me. You want it, you really do.

He tears me open. Tears me. Floods into me. I drown. I explode.

And it's going to happen again.


FROM II/SPACECO'S PROJECT ODYS-
SEUS SHOW:

(The face of Sirenaut Jane Voit, a nonde-script, nearly androgynous woman from the United States of America. There is no ex-pression on her face. Her colorless eyes seem not to see.)

JANE VOIT: Yes. I feel something. It's rather . . . nice.

MISSION CONTROL: High zapware ac-tivity indicated.

JV: Yes. I know. I feel it.

(Her face twitches. Her irises dilate, con-strict, then dilate again.)

MC: Jane? Jane?

* * *

WILLA: After we saw Jane Voit's attempt, we couldn't talk. We Sirenauts on the *Mothra* never talked to each other after the Odysseus show. But I could pick up those thoughts and feelings. . . .

Those zapware deaths were becoming our property. Each one made us feel a little more doomed. We all saw each other as the walking dead.

Pablo's fear feelings were mixed with his lust images of me.

I wished I could tell him what would happen. What always happens.

I wished I could resist his yearning to flow into me.

I wished I didn't want so much to flow into him.

Soon I let him touch me.

And it happened. The way it always happens . . .

Ay, this niña negrita went berserkísimo— I thought she was going to kill me. It was a pulsating paradise.

Then she went limp, like her brain stem was severed from her spinal cord. The Panther Woman melted into Raggedy Ann, who seemed to be stuffed with a soft, icy cold goo. I thought I had killed her.

First I gently patted her, whispering,

"Wake up, mi vida," into her ear. Then I slapped her a few times. No reaction. Nada.

She had a weak pulse and slow, lukewarm breaths were oozing out of her.

I made an emergency call.

MEDICAL EMERGENCY REPORT BY DR. MAGDA KOSCINA:

Willa Shembe is suffering from a form of telepathic neural overload, a rare condition particular to people with telepathic abilities. It can be triggered by the telepath being in crowded areas, closeness to individuals with violent emotions, or as in Shembe's case, sexual intercourse.

The tendency toward neural overload in Shembe's case is particularly due to experimental treatments researchers at the University of Soweto gave her in an attempt to increase her telepathic abilities.

Telepathic neural overload first manifests itself in violent convulsive seizures, ending in loss of consciousness, extreme muscular relaxation, and slowdown of body functions into a comatose, near-death state.

Not much is known about this condition, cases being rare and it being only recently recognized by the medical community. According to the literature, victims sometimes recover in a short time; other times they remain in a coma until death.

For treatment, we can only provide

Shembe with intravenous feeding and basic life support, and wait.

I also strongly suggest keeping Pablo Cortez away from her.

## TRANSCRIPT OF A MEETING BETWEEN DR. GOROG AND PABLO CORTEZ:

CORTEZ: Is she okay?

GOROG: The condition has not changed.

CORTEZ: I didn't mean it, you know. No way did I want to hurt her. I didn't know this would happen.

GOROG: Neither did we. There was no mention of it in her files. We've done some checking with the University of Soweto; seems it happened to her once before, in her teens. Similar situation, only the man was a research scientist who was working with her. He was over twice her age and married. The incident was covered up to avoid a scandal.

CORTEZ: Can anything be done?

GOROG: Dr. Koscina suggests keeping you away from her.

CORTEZ: I said I didn't know. . . .

GOROG: Yes, yes, and she didn't tell us. That is not good. We would have had serious doubts about accepting her into the program if we did.

CORTEZ: Will she be kicked out?

GOROG: Maybe. Maybe not. She may not recover. She may miss too much training.

But then, if she does recover—it is funny how this telepathic neural overload has many things in common with zapware death—it may be the thing that will allow her to survive a Siren encounter.

CORTEZ: Please, make sure they take care of her. And let me know if there's anything I can do to help. I really mean it!

Then it was as if I was in some sort of comacito—a weird sort of zombie/umkhovu-type walking coma. The person that made this trip livable was on a bed with tubes and wires sticking out of her. They wouldn't even let me see her. All I wanted was to sit there and hold her hand, but Koscina thought that would be too much for Willa's tortured nervous system.

So I caught on to the popular zombification among the Sirenauts. There was no going back—Jupiter was months away, Earth was almost a year away. The contracts were signed, we were all going to face the Sirens—alone. And from the way the Odysseus show was going, we were all going to die.

Sure, there was a kind of camaraderie. Even romances of convenience—I ended up seeing a lot of Ms. Aboid; but funny, I don't even remember what that chica's real name was.

\* \* \*

**INTERVIEW WITH ELIZABETH REGAN FROM** *EX-LOVES OF THE RICH AND FAMOUS:*

REGAN: It really rips me up that he doesn't even remember my name! But then he was always a bit distant and self-absorbed. Even when we were doing it, it was like his head was somewhere else. It's not like he was the greatest lover I've had—far from it—but I thought we did some good by each other! And all he can call me is "Ms. Aboid." What an insult! I should start calling him Señor Greaser!

We were like the god imitators that Aztec priests would choose for important sacrifices—we wear the prestige and privilege of being considered more than mere humano, but, hijolé, can you ever get the thought of the coming momento of truth out of your head, when that blade comes to cut out your heart?

And since there wasn't much else to do, I really got into the training. Once you gave in to it, endless sessions in the simulator and exercising in double-G wasn't so bad—it exhaustísimoed the body and numbed the mind and made time seem to slide by un poquito faster.

**PROGRESS REPORT ON PABLO CORTEZ BY DR. MAGDA KOSCINA:**

Cortez has ended his resistance and is now fully cooperating with his training. He has made a great deal of progress in the last few weeks, as expected, because he was in good health in the first place. His change in attitude has been a key factor in his progress.

This attitude change may have some negative effects. The withdrawal from social interaction that has been common to all the Sirenauts is worse in Cortez. Guilt over the incident with Shembe may be a factor. I don't feel that his emotional withdrawal is a good thing, and have told Dr. Gorog to pay close attention to him.

Then I'd dive into el sketchbook and draw my brains out. It helped me sort myself out—then again, it always has.

Willa's image faded from those drawings. I'd just take a crayon and do some savage slashes all over the paper, throwing lines around, letting it all dance to the rhythms that were beating deep in my tripas.

Then something would appear in the nonobjective scribble and I'd start drawing it, bringing it out. It was kind of like some of the techniques the original surrealists developed a century ago when they were trying to explore the unconscious mind—only Breton would have excommunicated me for some of the stuff I was doing, putting me in all kinds of good company—and a bit like the improvisation working of jazz, or tele-voodoo without the software, and what I do when working out the Siren images as they blast through my mind.

But those *Mothra* drawings were differ-ent, more influenced by what I was feeling at the time. Mis emociones. My ego. Me.

## PSYCHOLOGICAL REPORT ON PABLO CORTEZ BY DR. MUHAMMUD ALI GOROG:

I managed to convince Cortez to let me examine his sketchbooks. I thought I'd have to do some persuading, but he was more than happy to let me look at them. He ap-parently gets great satisfaction from people looking at his artwork.

In the beginning he seemed to be ob-sessed with Willa Shembe, but now seems to be filling page after page with violent, skeletal forms suggestive of death, preda-tors, eroticism: women's breasts, teeth, skulls, and sharp objects are seen over and over.

The style is gestural and expressionistic, with lots of repetitive and extraneous lines and very little open, or negative, space; sim-ilar to the horror vacui found in the draw-ings of institutionalized mental patients.

When I informed him that I found these drawings rather disturbing, he seemed pleased, revealing a sadomasochistic delight in shocking others.

This would all be purely academic if it weren't for the fact that his compulsive drawing has replaced all forms of social interaction, and members of both the *Mothra* crew and the other Sirenauts have expressed fear of him.

But then, who knows what sort of mind will be able to survive contact with the Sirens?

And somehow, to make it all worse, Willa recovered. Soon she was back with the rest of us Sirenauts, training like mad and trying not to get too close.

She and I didn't say una word to each other. We couldn't even bring ourselves to look at each other for the rest of that long, tediousísimo voyage to Jupiter.

It's hard to imagine that now. Things are so different. I feel her inside me. I see her all the time.

But that's getting ahead of things.

Next question, por favor?

# = 5 =

## IEAT

Sorry Anna, I just keep losing it. I've been this way since I've been Sirenized. My cabeza ain't completely my own anymore. Zapware televoovoo à la Sirens. I hate it at times; I've got this ego, El Señor Artista Quetzalcoatlian Prince! But now I'm no longer on my own.

It calls me: the paint, Willa, the Sirens, the images—*(Starships that grow on a tree that grows in deep space, nourished by cosmic radiation—portraits of faces, more like landscapes or furniture, so why do I know that they're faces?—schematics for technologies that work beyond quantum physics)*—then it all turns back into the paint that I'm smearing around with my fingers, melting into my technique and imagination and then there's Willa . . . everywhere . . . that Zulu beauty . . . that invisible, all-seeing mind's eye . . . zapping around through my neurons ... el universo ... the song of the Sirens.

Kind of like Odysseus or Ulysses or whatever you call him—whenever you call him—tied to a mast, unable to move, his ears open to the maddening song—only with me I'm stuck with a mad genius artist persona/egoísimo that suits alien purposes that nobody understands.

What am I saying? Alien? This is *their* place. Like, whaddaya mean *we*, white man?

Somebody actually called me white once. In Mexico. An Indio. At first I thought he was estúpido. It twisted my brains out of my eye holes. Like when some paddy would call me a nigger.

All right. Okay. I'm in control again. What was that you were asking me about, Anna baby?

So after nearly a couple of years, the meat of the midtwenties gone by, we finally reached Ithaca Base. It was one of the few times that all us Sirenauts all thought and felt united. We were todo eager to kiss *Mothra* and Koscina and Gorog and the double-G wheel and the simulator goodbye. Yeah, I know, mass stupidity, we should have known better—what else happens when too many minds agree on something? After our hitch on *Mothra*, we all figured we'd be overjoyed to be anywhere else, but unfortunately, Ithaca wasn't much of an improvement.

From watching the Odysseus show we had the idea—like the rest of the System still has, qué tontos!—that Ithaca was some kind of flashy, media paradiso; but unfortunately that turned out to be just the sets where they do the show. The rest of it looks like some kind of technophile slum that should be clipped onto the outskirts of Hightown any day now if we all don't look out. Mira: ugly walls with functional stuff sticking out, painted pukey-moco colors that some deranged psychiatrist decides would make living in such a mess tolerable.

It reminded me of the housing projects, shopping malls, and other SoCal Beautiful-ized parts of the L.A. sprawl—ugly things in gaudy colors with plants and flowers in unlikely places, and if you looked real close you'd see if the greenery was natural or artificial. When are people gonna learn that this kind of pasted-on-smile environment just makes for lotsa locos after a while?

So all us Sirenauts would growl, glazed eyed, get antsy until we end up fighting and/or et sextera and win some free tranquilizers.

Then there were these editorials about the inhumanity of this más cruel and unusual way of life, worse than, say, that of some naked kids playing in a Mudball jungle whose only choice for un futuro will be to aid and abet in destroying their homeland for a limited credit card that'd buy a few cheap thrills in an instamall before an early death due to unsafe working and living conditions.

EDITORIAL/PROMO BY NORBERT STARLING PRESENTED BY NORBERT STARLING MEDIA ENTERPRISES:

(In tight close-up, a little bald man with cobalt blue eyes, a bulbous nose, and a bristling mustache says:)

Norbert Starling here.

What about Project Odysseus?

Is it the highest achievement of science and civilization?

Or is it a new low in contemporary decadence that is corrupting science, entertainment, and the human spirit?

Will watching the weekly sacrifice of Sirenauts bring on a moral zapware death to the entire System?

I think so. That's why I, Norbert Starling, am taking the Norbert Starling Media Enterprises crew to Ithaca Base to find out what kind of twisted minds run such an operation—and even more startling, what kind of minds volunteer to have their brains sucked dry by the Sirens!

Coming soon to a network near you!

* * *

So pronto we were watching a tape of a muy importante message from that craggy-faced, bushy-browed, leader of the Project himself. . . .

## PROJECT ODYSSEUS IN-HOUSE MESSAGE FROM LUCIO CALVINO:

Sirenauts, no doubt you have been hearing some of the harsh criticisms of this project that have been filtering through the media.

Ay, ése, as if there was much else for us to do!

LC: Considering these criticisms and the impending arrival of Norbert Starling to do an exposé on Odysseus, I have decided to make some changes in the Sirenaut section that will not only improve our image, but lift the general morale as well.

Sí, señor, el gigante morale problema was so big you couldn't go anywhere on Ithaca without inhaling it, but of course the main office guys would never admit to the existence of such a chingadeda.

LC: What I am proposing is an Individual Encounter Approach Tactic program—IEAT, if you will—in which each of you will develop your own means of mental and emotional preparation based on individual personality and abilities, to give more of a fighting chance toward survival in a Siren encounter.

Yeah, yeah, all it was doing was making what was originally informal formal; and it would give us all some busywork with the space bureaucracy looking over us and trying to keep a lid on the general locoization, or at least the boredom—guess they figured busy loonie tunes were easier to handle than bored sickitos.

It wasn't long before IEAT got unofficially changed to EATME. Calvino referred to it as an allusion to *Alice in Wonderland*, which was news to us Sirenauts who were too busy arguing over who came up with it first to care about ancient Anglo literary allusions.

And don't let anybody fool you; *I* was the first one to call IEAT, EATME. Honest.

Anywhat, my IEAT, EATME, tres cojones, whatever, was based on—surprise! surprise!—painting. Heh, heh! My clever way of making them requisition the space and supplies for me to satisfy the image-making urge with more than just sketchbook scribbling. Of course, they wouldn't set up a splatterpainting studio for me—not yet, not then. Like, I wasn't no god yet, just a sacrifice-in-waiting. But I did get the stuff to make my cellito into a midget painting studio, where I could sling wet pigment to my heart's content—only in pseudograv it all had that sickening tendency to all drip in the same direction: down—so I had to keep twisting and turning the canvases ... all just for mumboing a little jumbo about how I figgeroo'd this'd help me avoid zapware death. ...

## IEAT PROPOSAL BY PABLO CORTEZ:

Ay! What is this zapware death the Sirens do on us 'nauts anyway, mis éses? It's the mind getting yanked out of the brain, into the Sirens' Big Red Synaptic Center. We all see it on the show every week; the Sirenaut always goes soft, opens up, lets go, and is gone, gone, gone.

Well, Pablo Cortez don't intend to let that happen to this cabeza. There's too much artist/genius going on here to be wasted.

And it's that artistic genius that I'm gonna use to beat the Sirens. I'm a collector and creator of images—it's what I've been training myself almost thirty years now to be. I plan on using this crazed brain as a computer system to scan what the Sirens are zapping out my way, grab it, and bring it back alive. I'm gonna hang on to my mind because I want to use it to paint what I see in Sirenland.

Of course, I'm going to need to do a lot of

painting to keep my brain in the painting/image-capture mode. . . .

So, by the time Señor hyperactive Norbert Starling arrived at Ithaca from the asteroid belt where he had just revealed to the System the exploitation of miners through consumer sex and drugs, the Sirenaut slum was a multiring circus of frantic activity that just begged to have cameras pointed at it: exercising, various techniques of meditation, electrostimulation of brains—a symphony of practice zaps, attitude and image focusing, praying, and even some things that made televoodoo and black magic look reasonable.

INTERVIEW BY NORBERT STARLING WITH DR. LUCIO CALVINO:
(Starling and Calvino walk down the halls of the Sirenaut living quarters.)
NORBERT STARLING: So this is where the Sirenauts live and spend most of their time. I must admit, it is—shall I say, colorful? How long has it had this rather ... unique paint job?
LUCIO CALVINO: Since immediately after construction. Spaceco's psychological research section has found that such a color scheme has beneficial effects on people who have to stay in one architectural environment for long periods of time.

NS: It looks an awful lot like the paint scheme I've seen in prisons all over the System.

LC: Yes. This type of paint scheme was originally tested in prisons, but for well over a decade now has been used in hospitals, factories, military bases—and living quarters in space facilities.

NS: But then why are all these doors closed? This all looks a lot like a prison to me. . . . Perhaps death row, with all the prisoners awaiting execution?

LC: So you finally found a place where you could figure in that comparison? It's striking, but it simply doesn't apply in this case. These doors are closed simply because the Sirenauts like their privacy.

NS: Could it also be a sign of the severe withdrawal that has been reported about the Sirenauts?

LC: It really isn't all that severe; and it's not a unique phenomenon, either. People working in dangerous jobs where they work alone and death is likely.

NS: But in this case death is certain.

LC: There is no proof of that.

NS: What about everyone who's been sent down to the Sirens dying—without exception?

LC: But we aren't yet sure what causes zapware death.

NS: Shouldn't the fact that it happens be enough?

LC: Not for science.

NS: But isn't this more show biz than science? After all, Spaceco is working with Interplanetary Infotainment on this project, and everyone knows that II works on a formula of a little bit of info combined with a lot of entertainment?

LC: I wouldn't know. I work for Spaceco. The only contact we have with II is through the funding they provide.

NS: But why would an outfit like II fund something like Project Odysseus if they didn't think they'd be making megabucks by entertaining their morbid, thrill-seeking audience?

LC: Again, I don't know about Interplanetary Infotainment's motivation, but they are doing a great service to science by providing us with funding.

NS: But aren't you demeaning science by turning research into a death show?

LC: The purpose of the Odysseus show is not to provide morbid entertainment, but to give the public a chance to experience Project Odysseus in detail.

NS: All the gory details? Like the zapware death of a Sirenaut a week? Are you even trying to arrange for at least one Sirenaut to survive?

LC: Believe me, Mr. Starling, that is one

of our primary concerns here—the eventual survival of a Sirenaut. If it were proved that Siren encounters were unsurvivable, I would be the first to suggest the elimination of the Sirenaut program. Meanwhile, we've started the Individual Encounter Approach Tactic, or IEAT, program, in which Sirenauts are working to develop methods that could let them survive.

NS: Has it helped?

LC: Well, we know that no Sirenaut has survived as of yet, but for months now IEATs have been used, are being cyberanalyzed and compared so that a workable survival method may eventually be developed.

NS: But until then there'll be more media-covered deaths and a shotgun approach to science.

LC: I have to remind you, we are dealing with a totally alien life-form: a complicated unknown with factors and a makeup we don't understand. There is no precedent for much of what we are attempting.

NS: Hmm. Very interesting. I suppose. So what about this IEAT program? What does it consist of? Where is it taking place?

LC: In answer to your first question: the IEAT program differs from Sirenaut to Sirenaut. Each is encouraged to develop an IEAT according to his or her temperament and abilities.

In answer to your second question: it is

taking place here (he indicates the door along the corridor) in these rooms.

NS: Oh really? You mean if I were to arbitrarily knock on one of these doors, we'd catch a Sirenaut doing something to prepare for meeting the Sirens?

LC: Yes.

NS: Well, I can't resist that. Think I'll do it now. (He pauses, waiting for a reaction from Calvino.)

LC: Go right ahead.

NS (disappointed that Calvino hasn't objected): Okay, this one looks likely. (He knocks. There is no answer. He knocks again.) Hmm. Seems to be a lack of cooperation here!

LC (touches on the door's intercom and speaks into it): Willa? Ms. Shembe? Could we speak to you?

WILLA SHEMBE (through the intercom speaker): Yes, Dr. Calvino. Just a minute. (Soon the door opens; Willa Shembe, looking glassy-eyed, peeks out.) May I help you?

LC: Willa, this is Norbert Starling. He would like to know about your IEAT.

WS: Hello, Mr. Starling.

NS: Hi, Willa. Now just what is your IEAT?

WS: I plan to use my telepathic ability to communicate with the Sirens.

NS: Telepathy, eh? Isn't that interesting. So you can read minds?

WS: Why, yes.
NS: Can you read mine?
WS: Yes. And you should be ashamed.

Yeah, good ol' Starling got a lot of inter-esante footage. A sort of freak-show pre-view of all us Sirenauts conducting bizarre do-it-yourself rituals hoping that somehow the Sirens'd be appeased and they'd spare us. He got some good shots of me paint-ing—action, visual stuff to contrast with the usual talking-heads doc style. He seemed to see me as a visual-aid source until that day when the number for the next lucky Sire-naut was drawn out of an important com-puter's randomizing function.

Guess what? It was mine!

Of course then Norbert just had to do an in-depth interview with moi, un hombre on the edge of death.

I didn't know what to feel, but I did laugh a lot.

**INTERVIEW BY NORBERT STARLING WITH PABLO CORTEZ:**

**NORBERT STARLING:** For a man who most probably will be dead next week, you smile a lot.

**PABLO CORTEZ:** (laughs)

NS: And laugh too.

PC: Hey, I'm from East L.A., ése! Un vato loco.

NS: What?

PC: A crazy guy.

NS: I'd say that anybody who'd volunteer for this project would have to be crazy.

PC: People have been calling me crazy all my life. I'm kinda used to it.

NS: But you're an artist. You barely escaped jail, turned down a chance to work with SoCal Beautiful, got into trouble with the SCP. What motivates a guy who should be living in some fashionable art center to accept a death sentence?

PC: Death sentence? You talk like you've been locoized.

NS: But honestly, Pablo, you could be the darling of any art community, living the good life in any of the most luxurious environments that modern technology can create; but instead you are out here in the System's boondocks, orbiting in a Spartan can on the edge of Jupiter's dangerously radioactive magnetosphere, living like a condemned man. Why?

PC (laughing again): Hey, man, I've seen what you call the good life: in Hightown, the L.A. sprawl, and several Central American cities. Ay! That's not what I call la vida.

NS: Excuse me. La vida?

PC: The life, ése. Living. Making the most of you and what's around you. Sure the comfort zones of the System are fun, nice places to visit, but the life there starts to bore me fast—nothing but people trying to see how far they can get their heads up their own nalgas!

NS: Excuse me. Nalgas?

PC: You really are culturally deprived, Norbert!

NS: Do you mean that you actually prefer living the way you do?

PC: I won't say that it never drives me crazy, but I'm excited most of the time. And I got no regrets. Most people these days who get any money indulge themselves to death inside their entertainment systems. I've been places, seen things—done things. Now I'm out here on the very edge—the frontier of what some folks call civilization, and I got a date with the real live mysterious unknown. I'm really excited. I can hardly wait.

NS: But, realistically, you will probably be dead in less than a week.

PC: (more laughter) Hey, my parents were neo-Aztecs. I didn't grow up with the whitebread Judeo-Christian technoamericano view of death as judgment. There ain't no heaven or hell the way the missionaries tell it. Death is part of life, so much that there is no cosmic punishment center, no shame for living; but there is glory for the outstanding, and that I am. Outstanding.

NS: So you expect to go into some Aztec afterlife.

PC: No way. My folks were the neo-Aztecs,

not me. That all died with them and the unfinished script and storyboards for animated films based on Aztec mythology that
was my legacy. I'm an all-purpose heathen
devil. A televoodooid image/symbol terrorist.

NS: Are you prepared to die?

PC: I don't expect to.

NS: But everyone else who's been to encounter the Sirens has.

PC: But I'm not everyone else. I never go
along with the crowd. Ask anyone who's
ever known me. That alone should mean I'll
survive.

NS: I don't understand you at all. You
must be stupid.

PC: You must be a (deleted).

After that interview, good ol' Norbert was
looking forward to seeing me die. How dare
I refuse to be the helpless victim he needed
me to be for his doc? There ain't no fury
like that of crusader scorned.

And in the week before my encounter I
got serioso. Logged a lot of simulator time.
Painted furiously. Eventually ended up
spending hours in an observation deck,
staring at a magnified view of the Great Red
Spot, burning those swirling clouds with
my mind, painting pictures out of the cloud
shapes inside my skull. Seeking the images,
capturing them, storing . . .

Deep down, I admitted to myself that I didn't want to die.

Gimme la vida! Life! Life! More life!

And soon it was time.

Soon I was stripped naked; like a handsome young Aztec boy, who, after being chosen by the priests to be the impersonator, imitator, actor to play the part of Tezcatlipoca—that's Smoking Mirror in Nahuatl—the wizard/trickster god who whispers those bad, bad, badísimo ideas into your ear and makes you do those things you don't really want to do and just know ain't right; the boy gets dressed in the finest of clothes, gets put up in the temple, is fed the tastiest of foods, gets a beautiful woman every night, until . . .

They scanned me inside and out, tried to talk their way into my cabeza. I tried to hang on to what made me me. Harder. Harder all the time.

Finally, I was in the ready room, the techies wiring and dressing me—like an Aztec god impersonator, only instead of jeweled, feathery finery, I get the latest, lightest, skintight, monitor-filled body sheath. Makeup was applied to my face so I'd look bonito for the cameras. The exoskeleton, to help me in la lucha against Jovian gravity, was clipped on, hooked up, activated. I was then handed over to the nimble claw machines that picked me up and fed me into the dirigiscaphe—while my Aztec counter-part would be marched up the pyramid and laid out on a crusty stone altar, his chest bared by the unwashed priests, the filthiest and stinkiest of whom would take a cere-monial flint blade that was damn-near laser sharp and open him up like a skilled sur-geon, exposing his beating heart, that is soon clutched in a grimy hand, cut from the body, and held up as it still beats to the god Tezcatlipoca to eat.

But in the mindset of the Aztecs, the boy *was* Tezcatlipoca. Some Anglo anthropolo-gist said that primitive peoples thought the performer to actually be what he was play-ing in rituals and even drama—like the same thing doesn't happen in the modern world of masscom entertainment. What makes you think you're so civilized, any-way?

The stage was set.

This ritual was beginning.

It was showtime!

FROM THE II/SPACECO ODYSSEUS SHOW OF PABLO CORTEZ'S ENCOUN-TER:

(Leon Wagner fades in to the Odysseus show set.)

LEON WAGNER: Well, II-ers and Spa-ceco fans, tonight, a change of pace, a Sire-naut with an artistic IEAT, Pablo Cortez.

He's painted his way from the graffiti underground of the L.A. sprawl, to Hightown, to Ithaca Base. And tonight—who knows where he'll end up after he enters the realm of the Sirens. Here's a clip from an interview I did with him just before the final suit-up. . . .

(Wagner fades out, leaving the view of Jupiter in the background, which fades to a magnified view of the Great Red Spot from an observation deck, with Pablo in the foreground.)

PABLO CORTEZ: I'm not sure how I feel. I'm excited. Anxiousísimo. Maybe a little nervous. I guess what I really feel like is a young man chosen by Aztec priests to impersonate the god Tezcatlipoca: honors and attention are heaped on, now I'm going to be suited up, exoskeletonized, made up, and then it's on with the ritual. El todo System is watching. They made me a star—with a leap of faith I could become a god.

(Cut to a view of both Wagner and Cortez.)

LW: Is this turn-of-the-century neo-Aztecism part of your IEAT?

PC: In a way, I guess. I was raised on it, so it's always there below the surface, but to me it's more like an atheist saying "oh my God" as a reflex. What I really believe in is me, and painting. Me the painter. Pablo Cortez. I'm going to start painting in my head the second I hit Siren-rich airspace and force myself to live to put it all on canvas—or whatever surface is available.

LW: Well, you seem confident enough. And the entire System wishes you luck.

PC: Yeah, I've been a pretty lucky muchacho—so far.

Okay, okay. I had my doubts. Inside I was a quivering blob. The god-imitator metaphor haunted me as I wore the exoskeleton like Aztec plumes and the dirigiscaphe was lowered. This was not a simulation—it was real. El realismo muy grande y serioso. It was like marching up a pyramid to bare my chest to a jagged blade. It was a ritual.

I took some deep breaths—what they told us to do in training—and took control, made it into *my* ritual. I was ready to drop my brain into the synapse-storm of the Sirens, paint pictures in my head, hang on to my nervous system and . . .

(Fade back to Wagner on the set.)

LW: So Dr. Calvino tells me that Pablo is entering the Great Red Spot, so let's switch to our live feed from the dirigiscaphe. . . .

(Fade to Pablo, encrusted in the exoskeleton, inside the dirigiscaphe.)

LUCIO CALVINO (voice-over on intercom): Do you feel anything yet?

PC: If only those bastards could go through this. They should all come up here and see this planetísimo up close before they call me undisciplined!

LC: What are you talking about?

PC: Este sight! Jupiter up close! Wagstaff and the rest of los tontos at the SCP should see *this*, that is what space art should be all about! This energy! This power! This freedom! Este es what I had in mind when I created splatterpainting!

LC: What about the Sirens? Are you feeling any effects?

PC: En mi cabeza? No. This gravity is a bitch, though. If only I could see these clouds while weightless! If only I could come here and paint—really paint, outside of my head with the paint flying! Can't they build one of these exoskeletons with more freedom of movement?

LC: The one you have is the state of the art. The instruments show that you are in a Siren-rich area. Do you feel anything yet?

PC: Yeah, now that you mention it. The gravity. Gravitísimo. It's getting hard to breathe. . . .

LC: Should we abort?

PC: No! I'm feeling bueno now. Lighter. The gravity seems to be going away. I almost feel weightless. It's really great! Feels like I could peel this exoskeleton right off—

LC: Don't!

PC: I'm not estúpido, Calvino! It's probably an illusion—like what happened to the others. I'm doing my EATME—I mean IEAT now. I do plan on surviving this!

LC: Any change in sensations?

PC: Hijolé! One long rush. Ecstasy—like I'm weightless, or painting away like crazy—making a big, juicy messísimo! I'm getting an erection. The exoskeleton is holding me down.

Then I got this strong rotten-eggs whiff of methane. I painted a planetwide sewer in my mind, then thought, Hey? Could the dirigiscaphe be leaking? Then there was that microlightning, all over—kind of tickled. I was about to say something, but couldn't move, nada movemento—first I was paralyzed, every muscle locked tight, then it all turned to mush—flesh, bones, exoskeleton, dirigiscaphe, Jupiter, Ithaca Base, the whole galaxy. . . .

LC: Cortez, are you all right?

I was getting softer—like a Salvador Dalí watch. Everything was getting soft and squishy. Putty. Liquid. Gas. Like those colorful, flowing clouds that were all around turning into impossible mind's eye planet-wrapper paintings of stuff that amazed me but I couldn't figure out.

LC: Pablo, are you there?

* * *

I was a twisting, bubbling cloud—dancing among the gorgeous clouds of Jupiter—among microscopic creatures I couldn't see, but could feel; like spirits, like ghosts, like loas.

LC: Abort! Abort!

I felt that I was dissolving. Being absorbed. I panicked.

Then they had me. *Me.* Who never gives in to anybody.

I passed from the realm of Xiuhtecuhtli—el supreme being within space and time, the power of life and fire, the center of all things and spindle of the universe—to Omeyocan, the realm of Ometcuhtli, the male/female supreme being, the dual lord, source of all existence, the essential unity in difference. Spacetime was flushed down the toilet—a cute cartoon Einstein offered himself as a blood sacrifice. A kind of electric dreamtime.

And somewhere, when I was aware of the dirigiscaphe's engines burning and the G's building up so that even the exoskeleton couldn't save me from harm.

(Cut to Leon Wagner on the set.)
LW: Well, it looks like another brave

Sirenaut has fallen victim to zapware death. . . .

(He suddenly brings a hand to the tiny implant in his right ear.)

Wait. What's this?

(He smiles.)

Science fans, I am happy to report that Pablo Cortez is alive! He has sustained broken bones and internal injuries from the emergency escape burn, has not regained consciousness, but there is brain activity!

A Sirenaut has survived contact!

This changes everything!

Like Leon's quote that was soon all over the media in every possible form, it really did change everything. Todo cambio, éses. Future encounter attempts were suspended. The attention of Project Odysseus and the media-hungry System was turned to me, my coma, and the possibility of bringing me out of it.

Even Norbert Starling decided to stick around, hoping this was the end of the project and I'd somehow give him a juicy ending for his doc.

I'm really sorry I missed it, but then the Sirens and trying to keep a death grip on my life was keeping me busy.

# = 6 =
## Coma

So, hija, I showed them. I didn't die. I survived, because I'm mad enough to see it all
without going mad. Because my imagination is powerfulísimo enough to face what
most people find unthinkable.

I wallowed in it, dreamed eye-frying pictures of it all that would prove my genius
to everyone, and make the ghosts of Diego
Rivera, Siqueiros, Orozco, and every vato
who scrawled his name on a wall proud of
me.

But it didn't end. Just went on and on and
on. Image after mind-nuking image. I was
totally delighted! Flow and endless stream
of bizarre imagery before my eyes and I'm
in some kind of paradiso. It was like—no,
better than staying up all weekend loco
watching your local all-horror-movie channel. Like a rolly-wet amor-make with that
sculptress who was disgusted when I
glooped all over her work.

Like after I was still culture-shocked at my tía's house just months after my parents died when they gave me that package of the script and storyboards for turning Aztec myths into cartoons that Madre and Padre were working on—and never finished. I stared at it all for days, became determined to learn to read and draw, to make them proud of me, and, maybe, somehow make them come back. I fell in love with the Aztecs—after all, I looked like one of them, and for the first time I realized that I was handsome, even beautiful—and was delightísimoed that these bloodthirsty, cannibalistic, colorful monsters were *mine*, not property of the light-skinned aliens from "back east"—they were *my* heritage, it was *my* blood that stained those pyramids, *my* art that survived the campaign of another Cortés centuries ago, so powerful that it took Western art until the twentieth century to catch up.

Like all this was something I dreamed up and was damn proud to have such a fantastic imagination!

FROM WILLA SHEMBE'S DIARY:

Yes, everything has changed.

I should have known that about Pablo. That he would change everything. Especially with the help of the Sirens.

I wish I could have been in his mind. . . .

If I could be in his mind now . . .

It's why I volunteered. I need minds to read. It is a hunger. It drives me. My desire.

All I want is to see it all. Let everything pass through my mind. No more bodies. No more experiments. Just all the images in the universe.

I always wanted to be an invisible spirit, seeing everything.

I have a strong feeling that the Sirens can do this for me. Even if it kills me.

Pablo, I feel you have cheated me. Why did you have to be so selfish that they stopped the encounters?

I want my turn.

I find myself wishing to be inside your mind again.

## PROJECT ODYSSEUS REPORT BY DR. LUCIO CALVINO:

Six weeks and Pablo Cortez is still comatose. Reports from II and Spaceco subtly express impatience. The audience of the Odysseus show doesn't seem to be satisfied with redundant reports on Cortez's condition and the presentation of theories about why he survived and what it could mean about the nature of the Sirens. I feel pressured to begin the weekly encounter attempts again.

And that is something I cannot do. That would be more show business than science—and I can't bring myself to verify that accusation. We are here to find out about the Sirens; so far the bloody media show that has supported us has been a side effect—I won't let it take over.

Pablo's injuries are returning to normalcy. The doctors disagree if his coma is zapware-induced. There is a great deal of brain activity.

Something will have to be done soon. Once again we are on unknown ground. There is no procedure for me to fall back on. All I have are a few random bits of data, a little logic, and my imagination.

FOOTAGE FROM NORBERT STARLING MEDIA ENTERPRISES:

(Close-up of Pablo's face, unnaturally pale, beard now full, more of his hair has gone gray. He has tubes coming out of his nose and arms. Monitors are attached to vital areas. His eyes jerk around irregularly, much like REM sleep.)

NORBERT STARLING (offscreen): Well, here he is. Pablo Cortez, the System's newest hero, the subject of all the fashionable talk you've been hearing lately. Take a look, take a good look.

(As Starling pauses, the camera remains fixed on Pablo's face, which does not move except for an occasional eye twitch.)

It doesn't look like much is happening here to me.

(The camera pulls back to show Starling standing beside the bed and the readout screen in the background.)

Sure, these gadgets show that his body is minimally functioning, and there's some strange activity sparking away in his brain; but if you ask me, it all looks awfully pitiful.

A few weeks ago I interviewed Pablo Cortez. It was no big deal. He was just another Sirenaut getting ready for a mission, maybe a bit less of a bore because he was rather energetic and eccentric and his painting made some refreshing visual counterpoint to the usual headtalk, but I could say one thing for the kid—he was alive and lively. But then nobody really cared outside of his being a Sirenaut.

Now he can't talk. He can't even wake up. And you Systemfolx have made him your most popular celebrity, your favorite vegetable.

Frankly, it makes me sick.


A REPORT BY LUCIO CALVINO:

I believe that I may have found something to do about the Pablo Cortez situation that will satisfy the pressures to put on another Odysseus show and may even give us the breakthrough we need.

In going over the files on the training of Cortez aboard the *Mothra*, I found that he had a relationship with another Sirenaut—one Willa Shembe. Shembe is a telepath with abilities that have been documented, even in an incident involving Cortez.

What I propose is to have Shembe attempt to read Pablo's mind. This should give the II people a media event they can show, and maybe knock our research out of the frustrating doldrums that we've been locked into.

FROM WILLA SHEMBE'S DIARY:

I was having a dream.

Pablo came to me, still with the wires and tubes sticking out of him. He touched me, overloading me again. I was scared, but also felt delighted. Words are inadequate here. Images are better. And feelings.

I woke up in a cold sweat, breathing hard. I was glad it was a dream, and it was over, but still . . .

Pablo . . . I'm afraid of him. I am also drawn to him. His touch. His mind. It would be so much.

Then the intercom buzzed. It was Dr. Calvino. He wanted to see me.

I asked if it was about Pablo.

He said yes.

I felt as if I was back in the dream again.

* * *

# FROM A MEETING BETWEEN DR. LUCIO CALVINO AND WILLA SHEMBE:

CALVINO: So, Willa. Will you be willing to do this for us?

SHEMBE: I don't know. I think so. I would like to read Pablo. Though I am afraid. I guess what I am saying is that I will try.

CALVINO: Very good, Willa. I want you to approach this as you would an experiment for the department of parapsychology at the University of Soweto.

SHEMBE: Yes. But I hope it won't be as unhappy as in those times.

CALVINO: How much preparation do you think you'll need?

SHEMBE: I could do it right now.

CALVINO: It won't be that soon. We have to get a show planned.

SHEMBE: Couldn't it be private?

CALVINO: I'm afraid not. It will have full media coverage, like a Siren encounter.

SHEMBE: I understand. It's just that my feelings for Pablo are so . . .

CALVINO: Don't worry, we're counting on those feelings being a big help.

SHEMBE: How strange. For me my own feelings have always been trouble.

So Señor Dr. Calvino had a brainstorm—not as explosive as the storm in my own gray matter, but more inspiration than I thought could ever happen behind those bushy eyebrows of his. He fixed me up on a date with Willa—and arranged for el todo System to watch.

If I knew it was happening, I'd've been anxious. Never could wash Willa out of my mind. All the Sirenaut busywork helped to keep me from sneaking a visit and risking sending her into telepathic neural overload again.

I'd've been smiling—if the Sirens weren't running all this other stuff through my cabeza.

# = 7 =

## Sirenland

Gee, I just don't know, Anna. It all might have been like a long dream or hallucination, but, ay—it was all being fed directly into my mind, brain, cabeza or whatever—the religiosos are throwing around the words "soul" and "spirits," the scientists are sticking with zapware—so for me it was all realísimo. Sure, I was aware that just outside Jupiter's magnetosphere, in Ithaca's hospital section, my body was lying there with all these tubes and wires stuck into it, recovering from a concussion, a ruptured spleen, and an assortment of broken bones. But somehow it didn't seem that importante. Sure, I was Pablo Cortez, but the struggle to keep me inside me soon got easy—I could do it with less than half my brain, and my musclebound ego. At the same time I was in so many other places. . . .

I was also being born. I was dying. Often.

I was alive and well and living millions of years ago on Mars.

My body and its suffering were just part of the Sirens' show.

Like pentasexual orgies in sparkling caverns or sonic wars in oceans that flowed through endless gigantic tubes or zapware epic chants of a silicon-crystal disc jockey.

Et cetera . . .

## II/SPACECO ODYSSEUS SHOW SPECIAL: WILLA SHEMBE'S ENCOUNTER WITH PABLO CORTEZ:

(Leon Wagner at the Odysseus show desk. This time, instead of the Great Red Spot, an extreme close-up of Pablo Cortez's closed, occasionally twitching eyes are bluescreened into the background.)

LEON WAGNER: Greetings at long last, II-ers and Spaceco fans! It's been a while, I know we've all been itching for a new Odysseus show, hanging on any news about Pablo Cortez's condition, but especially yearning for a new encounter.

Well, tonight we have something different. An encounter of sorts—but not one in which a Sirenaut rides a dirigiscaphe down into the Great Red Spot. This time Lucio Calvino has thought of a way to have a Sirenaut perhaps encounter the Sirens, and maybe cause a change in Pablo's condition. Dr. Calvino has decided to send Sirenaut

Willa Shembe—who has telepathic abilities—on an encounter with, not the Sirens, but Pablo!

This is new territory we're entering. No telling what will happen. It should be exciting.

But first, what about Willa Shembe? Who is she and why was she chosen for this special mission?

Well, I talked to her earlier and here's a portion of that conversation:

(Cut to Willa Shembe and Leon Wagner in a conference room.)

LW: So Willa, you're a telepath, eh?

WILLA SHEMBE: Yes.

LW: Have your abilities been documented?

WS: Yes. When I was younger, I was taken in by the parasychology department of the University of Soweto. I was the subject of many experiments.

LW: Was that around the turn of the century?

WS: Years after. I am not that old.

LW: But that would be during the early years of the Revolutionary Government, Zululand's New African Culture Program, so-called "native science." It was controversial in the rest of the world. Especially the parapsychological research.

WS: I wouldn't know. I was just a child. An experimental subject.

LW: Did you know Pablo before?

WS: Yes, we both came over on the *Mothra*.

LW: Is is true that the two of you got to be more than just friends?

(Shembe looks embarrassed, starts fanning herself.)

WS: We got to be very close.

LW: Did you ever have telepathic contact with him.

WS: Yes.

LW: Then that should help in your attempt to contact him now.

WS: Yes. Dr. Calvino and the others think so.

LW: Tell me, Willa. How did such a shy girl like you decide to become a Sirenaut?

WS: I like to read minds. I get hungry for it. Only most minds are so ... tedious, uninteresting. I thought the Sirens would be interesting. Something different.

LW: And was Pablo interesting, something different?

WS (smiles): Yes.


And what et cetera, ése! There was no space or time—Omeyocan all the way with superimposed flashes of stuff that wasn't quite tuned right so my nervous system could process it into any kind of information or imagery, but I gave it a good honest try and—ay! I heard the big beat of whales and dolphins in perfect sync with songs of sentient stars and the Sirens that toy robots and nude Betty Boops joyously danced to in endless halls that were covered with animated hieroglyphs that joined in the Futuro-Afro-pre-Columbian-Trans-Spacetime-Quantum Musical Comedy!

And no, no, no, I don't know what it all is and where it comes from—zapware dreamtime, I don't know! It was just there and real as anything you could plug into with your senses. First, just a scrambloso jumble like reality snapcracklepopping before my very eyes, ears, nose, mouth, and all those nervicito endings all over my brown skin. Made me feel like I was going to fall apart into a cloud of loose atoms, but I held on with all I was and tried to paint it all in the image lab behind my eyes. Then it started changing into things.

Flashes of . . . otherworldly stuff . . . like hyperloaded sci-fi . . . like this parade of idols hewn out of the hearts of neutron stars, hungrily marching through the cosmos to the galaxy where entire civilizations were offered as sacrifices and herds of armored, winged worms devoured planets and shit art and technology!

I'd get the feeling of being spread throughout the atmosphere of Jupiter in billiones of bits and pieces sparking connections in baby lightning making something that wasn't thoughts like we have them—more like receivers with omnidirectional antennae receiving simultaneous signals from sources all around, all over, then I was all around and all over.

The images would go from incoherent to incomprehensible to bizarre to familiar as I struggled to paint them in my cabeza:

Imageflashes, pictographoids—then, like thoughts, like memories, like dreams, all those otra senses start seeping in—a smell, a taste, a feel . . . sounds, voices even—old conversations rerunning and how do you paint a picture of that?

Back in SoCal, back in my childhood, I could hear my tía and tío "discussing" me:

"All he wants to do is look at that damned Aztec stuff!"

"Let him, vieja. It's all he has left from his parents."

"But it's heathen; and it eventually killed them."

"So we tell him that they died trying to accomplish something. And that it was honorable, something he can be proud of."

"But it's all so weird."

"Like them."

"I just don't know. I don't see how all this nonsense could be good for Pablito. It's against God."

"It's full of gods. What do you think all those feathered serpents and things are?"

Soon I'd see feathered serpents that would fly into the window of my tía's house and soon Quetzalcoatl and Tezcatlipoca were fighting their eternal battle in my old bedroom. Tlaloc would adjust his goggles and flood the place with storm clouds and lightning bolts like that cavernous thunderstorm I flew through on a gypsy plane to Mexico City—like the inside of the Great Red Spot. Coatlicue, the ravenous, serpent-skirted earth goddess came in and devoured everything.

It reminded me of my parents' unfinished Aztec mythology project, and then there were my parents, smiling at me. I ran to them, but they were always just out of my reach. And they wouldn't talk to me. Then I remembered, hey, loco, of course they can't talk—they're dead, fried their brains with ATL. Their flesh then crumbled away from their faces, revealing very Aztecan skulls underneath. Maggots wormed out of their remaining skin. Then, they began to move and handed me an old-fashioned video cassette labeled *Aztecan Mythotoons*. A huge, mouthlike wound opened over my heart. I shoved the cassette into it and saw my parents' finished project, as I always wanted to, and happily cried flying oceans as it all danced around through me in hyperamplified neurocyberanimation: the vast, intergalactic flying oceans all ran together, merged, and condensed into the primal mythical ocean that all was before the Creation of the One World when all was without form and void—to pillage the mythology of those who pillaged ours—when the earth-mother goddess Coatlicue was not yet She of the Serpent Skirt, but the Cipactli Monster, swimming, devouring—the serpent eating its own ever-growing tail; now whose mythology is that? Quetzalcoatl and Tezcatlipoca decide that things have to begin, attacking the monster, tearing her apart, separating the ocean from the sky from the land, creating the unique cosmology of the Aztecs that keeps flashing through me, the myth of violent creation like Pablo attacking a blob of paint in zero-G—Mama, Papa; see? see? I remember; I know. Fastforward through the first three suns under which earlier races of beings existed before man, but didn't please the gods, couldn't say the god names—so they were destroyed and Quetzalcoatl who had earlier transformed himself into a red ant—gods can do things like that—to deliver maize to the surface of the Earth—that's Earth capitalized, sacred—then as a man journeyed to Mictlán, the Land of the Dead, to bring the current human into existence by offering blood from his penis—takes más huevos than just getting yourself nailed to a cross— letting the sacred red fluid drop onto the

ashes of the last prehumans, infusing them
with life, making them into the first humans, our ancestors. Then in the Toltec city
of Tula Quetzalcoatl founded the basis for
all Mesoamerican cultures, creating a society like no other, that those that followed
looked to as an ideal of perfection for centuries. Tezcatlipoca didn't like the way his
brother Quetzalcoatl did things: all too tied
up in the concepts of purity, favoring the intellect and spirit over the physical world, the
body, desire—that was the Way of Fleshlessness. It was that denial of the caliente/
picante juiciness of existence and how it all
could feel so good and bad ... just plain
*feel* that was Quetzalcoatl's undoing; it allowed the wizards of Tezcatlipoca to use the
diabolical mood/mind-altering drug alcohol
in the form of the sacred drink pulque—
you know, made from the maguey plant
that can be refined into the milder stuff
called mezcal that in turn can be refined
into this even milder stuff called tequila—
to cause stodgy ol' Quetzalcoatl to have a
meltdown of his hypercoolísimo and have
him get it on with his sister, disgracing
himself, giving him no choice but to sail
southward on a raft of serpents to a place
called Tapallán, leaving the One World under the domination of Tezcatlipoca and his
cruel jokes and dirty tricks that influenced
and inspired Huitzilopochtli as he led the

Mexica, who are now known as the Aztecs from their original homeland of Aztlán, to the place where an eagle fought a snake on a cactus and the fabulous city of Tenochtitlán—nowadays known as Mexico City AKA Mexico, D.F.—capital of the Nahua/Mexica world was founded. There were fought the flowery wars, where the objective was not victory, but the collecting of prisoners to be sacrificed to the gods. It all grew bloodier and bloodier until strange portents and apparitions—a bird with a mirror for a head, men with two heads, and other strange beings that were seen, then vanished—foreshadowed the coming of the aliens with pale hairy faces who could become centaurs in battle. Montezuma was such a superstitious fool, mistaking that other Cortez—well, actually Cortés, before linguistic evolution did its number—but that happens when you come cara a cara with the unknown, the alien; I—we should know, just look at what the Sirens did to us . . . and it all becomes a big, barbaric, bloody battle—not a flowery war, in which all is ritual and the objective is capture, sacrifice, but a slaughter with spears, arrows, and obsidian-blade-edged clubs against metal swords and cannons. Blood and viscera saturate the dreamscape as blood, bodies, peoples run together in a primordial soup boiling with varied genetic materials and in that ocean I found me—Pablo Cortez, not the Ego That Was Art, but Pablito, the little boy with the big identity crisis. I came together like some Frankenstein monster out of bits of Spanish conquistador centaurs and Aztec Indian warriors.

Ah! Ay! Qué bueno, bellísima, mis padres! Gracias, muchísimas gracias, mamá y papá!

So what am I, Spanish or Mexican? Do I import my culture from Europe or try to piece together what was destroyed in the New World? Dare I create my own culture, be an American? Who do Americans insist on calling me a foreigner when my family spoke English generations before theirs did? Who gave my native continent that ridiculous Italianoid name anyway?

PC: Sorry. Got un poquito carried away there. It just starts flowing through me and I can't stop it. Hope I didn't lose you.

AP: Not at all. I'm fascinated by you, Pablo. The whole System is fascinated by you. We want to know all we can about you. We can't get enough.

(She smiles, her tongue passes over her teeth, flicking off a sharp canine.)

PC: Yeah. I know. It kinda scares me. I wonder if I can provide enough Pablo to satisfy el demando popular.

AP: You're doing a good job.

PC: Yeah. Maybe too good a job. Lucky this happened—that I ended up like this. All you have to do is slice me open and it all gushes out.

AP: Does this bother you?

PC: In a way.

(He swats a tiny sphere of paint, sending a fresh rain of splattermarks across his face.)

PC: I just wish that all you chingadoids weren't so hungry.


(Cut to Leon Wagner, live at his desk. Bluescreened in the background, a shot of Pablo's bed with Willa and Dr. Calvino standing in front of him.)

LW: So things are about ready to go here, so let's switch to the Ithaca Base hospital section, to join Willa and the ever-popular Dr. Calvino.

(Cut to the scene behind Wagner's desk.)

LW (offscreen): Willa. Dr. Calvino. Are you ready there?

(Willa nods.)

LUCIO CALVINO: Yes. As you can see, we have Willa wearing brainscan monitors. With Pablo also fully monitored we will be able to tell if any other-than-normal brain activity occurs and (he steps aside, revealing several uniformed med teamers standing around the bed) we have a medical team ready to handle any emergencies that may occur.

LW: You expect some kind of trouble?

LC: We don't know what to expect.

LW: Well, I'm sure our audience is anxious to see something. Shall we begin?

LC: Yes. Willa, approach Pablo.

(Willa nods and goes over to the bed, leans over, bringing her head close to Pablo's. The monitors show changes in both her and Pablo's brain-activity readings.)

Then I had flashes of women I'd known— "Ay, Pablito, you're so nasty," the niñita I balled as a sacrifice to Tlazolteotl, goddess of filth and depravity, "No please—ah, that feels so good," past midnight in an empty high-school campus on a hot SoCal night, "What if somebody comes and sees us? Oh! Do that again," she was all hot, soft, firm, young, warm flesh, "Ay! Ay! Ay! Pablito! Pablito! Pablito!"; the French college girl "très brutal, très sauvage, Pablo" I ran around those Mayan ruins "mon amor, I want us to be like l'humanité in the primeval state in this très elemental place" with as the napalm glow of the latest microwar flickered at the horizon "C'est dommage! Civilization encroaches!"; the Viet vixen "For the last time—you're just too weird! Too irresponsible! You just don't fit into my life!" that broke my heart real good; "But you love it. All this attention, and the fact that you're going places now. You love it more than you ever loved me," Estela; "I know . . . I can be a real flake at times ... but you know how it is to be a real artist here. If you don't keep in the media's mind you end up splashing down on the Mudball again ..." Firedrop; "G-day, Brown Eyes," Ms. Aboid ...

Then, slowly, not all at once, overlapping into what I've talked at you before, like a virus eating into the Sirens/Pablo mix. There are flashes of Africa: scenes of riots in a rat-infested packing-crate bantustan, not like the video newsflashes but out of the senses of a terrified young girl who could feel the turmoil of all the angry minds around chewing away at her brain, dissolving vague memories of parents she hardly knew. The taste of other minds on hers scared her, fascinated her, like the soft sound of a swishing skirt, the trademark of the umkhovu, the living dead—Willa trickled into my mind. Her memories trickled into me like infectious static: "You understand, Willa, that what happens in your mind isn't supernatural; it is a chance for our country to prove that it is modern and scientific. Also we need something to unite all the tribes and keep the white minority from succeeding in a counterrevolution. You can combine our ancient past with a glorious future. . . ." And the experiments— they seemed like torture to me, I mean her. And that cabrón who raped ... I could kill him, easily for what he did to us. Yet she was so eager to have something different to wrap her telepathic tendrils around.

Ay! I was jolted!

It was being outside of space and time with Ometcuhtli—then suddenly feeling the presence of Nkulunkulu, the Zulus' maker of all things. I was being manipulated by an unseen sangoma, a Zulu diviner with a cattle gallbladder crown and necklace of vials of herbs—no, rather an abathakathi, an evil wizard whose most important product is misery; killing, illness, and drought—making a diabolical potion out of pieces of a human body—me! I felt a phantom kiss where she bit off the tip of my tongue, left me animal-eyed and forever spooked—her umkhovu, slave to her magic, locked in her spell.

But I didn't know nada about the Zulus, their mythology or superstitions. What I did know Willa told me, and she ain't much of a talker. And now like the rest of the Sirens' song, as if I heard it all from living in a bantustan, it just flooded my skull, only more intense, only more, más: the taste of roast chicken and uputhu drowned out that of hot, greasy tacos and the bitter blood of long, crunchy caterpillars in my mouth! Experiments that she didn't understand—a continuing nightmare that made her want to retreat from the world and live through the images from other people's minds.

* * *

(Willa smiles, then moans with delight.)
LW: Well, at least she's having a good time here!

I was receiving mucho input from her mind, for a change. Not just her subdued body language and sparse words. And that bright, clear flashing of those big, brown eyes. Very interesante. She was a strange being, like humanoids who ride see-through ships to the end of time to observe the aesthetic qualities of the heat death of the universe. Other people's experiences, and thoughts, were what she lived for. She rarely ate, or moved, was more interested in reading more and more minds than the university's experiments. I remember it all as if it happened to me. I—I mean she, refused to eat. She wasted away. They thought she would die. Then through someone's mind she found out about the Sirens, and said some of her few words.

"Take me to them!"

(Willa collapses on top of Pablo, their faces touching. The instruments go wild.)
WS: Beautiful, I love it!
LW: What's this? The princess trying to wake our sleeping beauty with a kiss?
* * *

Ay! How she relished it. Devoured it greedily. Like Coatlicue giving birth and eating up the universe.

*My argument with Estela after the Guer-rilla Muralist "trial": "I never wanted to form any revolutionary art gang and get into all kinds of trouble. That was all something you dragged me into, because you wanted to show me off to your friends. All I wanted from you was a bit of good, honest romance, some tenderness and juicy amor on lonely nights. I'm good enough at getting into trou-ble on my own." "But you love it." Rainbow-filled skies over effervescent seas. My shedding my own blood like Quetzalcoatl did to revive the human race so I could have something to paint with in a ritual that I believed would bring my parents back to life when I was eight years old. Tía caught me, stopped me, zapped the hell out of me with an electric stun-spanker; I was mad at her because I knew the magic would work and she ruined it. The joy I felt the first time I was weightless, and decided that gravity was the enemy of true freedom and decided to splash my paint. A war of radioactive cloud beings that goes on for millennia across bil-lions of light-years. Cartoons I'd draw on my clothes when I got bored in school. Invisible beasts that flex gravity at will and eat black holes!*

She flowed into me and absorbed it all.

My memories. The Sirens' maelstrom-of-imagery song. My fantasies. My realities.

Then she tore through me and leaped into the Sirens.

(Willa's brainscan monitor goes straight-line. The emergency buzzer sounds. Pablo's eyes open.)

Suddenly it was like enough of my ego was stuffed back into my skull to let me use my body again. The zapware spacetime short circuitry got turned down. This was here/now, there/then.

For un momentito I could see clearly through my own eyes, and see me through her eyes, *and* watch the song of the Sirens with no eyes at all.

Then: *Cracko!* Something snapped. The deadly intensity in her eyes—that were almost touching mine—clicked off.

(The med team lifts her up, starts checking vital areas with fingers and instruments.)

MED TEAMER: She's dead.

I laughed. A lovely demonic laugh that took my my entire, aching body and all my strength. It hurt like hell and was worth it. They all, even Calvino—and the cameras—looked into my loco eyes.

\* \* \*

PABLO CORTEZ: Idiots! Fools! Estúpidos!

LUCIO CALVINO: You're alive!

(The med team swarms over Pablo.)

LC: What happened? How do you feel?

PC: Shut up! (He wrestles with the med teamers.) Get away from me! There's so much . . . I can't . . . Let me out of this. (He tries to get out of the bed, starts pulling off the IV tubes and monitor wires.)

LC: No! You're seriously injured!

So it hurt like a bitch—I didn't care, gritted my teeth, fought them off. Soon a few throat-rupturing banshee screams kept them at bay. The floor hit me like a macrocosm of pain. Damn gravity—even the centrifugal force, fake kind!

After a while they all just watched me with awe and dread as if I was a rotting corpse that suddenly sprang back to life. Luckily, my right arm was working; in a cast, but I could move it at the shoulder, where it counts. I reached under my gown and agonizingly tore off the hospital diaper.

LEON WAGNER: My God! What is he doing? How disgusting—but this is a, er, historic moment, Systemfolx. We owe it to science to show you this. Parents, however, may want to practice discretion. . . .

* * *

I needed something to paint with. Something that would smear and leave a mark. It had been years since I'd cacafinger-painted. It'd have to do.

And it did nicely.

Before los pendejos shot me with a sedative that knocked me out, I managed to smear one vision onto the floor.

# = 8 =

## *Pablomania*

After months of zapware hyperdream state, the sedation was actually rather refreshing—something un poquito like deep sleep, no alien image flashes roaring through my battered brain; just good, old, cold, numb unconsciousness. Whew!

If only I could have seen the holy havoc that was bubbling over all over the System. I'd've been amused.

But then I did need some rest.

FROM THE NORBERT STARLING SPECIAL REPORT ON WILLA SHEMBE:

(Close-up on the embalmed, heavily made-up face of Willa Shembe through the transparent viewplate of a metallic transport coffin.)

NORBERT STARLING (offscreen): So here she is—all packed away and ready to be loaded onto the next freighter to Earth.

An unmanned freighter. She's no longer a human being. She is a corpse. Cargo.

(The camera pulls back to show Starling standing over the coffin.)

One final indignity. Just like all the other Sirenauts before her, but with one important difference. . . .

(He puts his hand on the coffin.)

She never had an encounter with the Sirens. Her encounter was with another Sirenaut—Pablo Cortez, the man who survived the Sirens but has seemingly become deadly himself.

As I record this sequence, Pablo Cortez is being coddled by Spaceco's greatest scientists—behind locked doors—all because of a picture he drew with his own excrement! The System's media networks are making vicious deals to secure access to him. And you, Systemfolx, can't seem to find anything else to talk about these days.

(The camera zooms in to a close-up of Starling.)

People, it's an outrage. The woman in this coffin is dead. And her death was the result of contact with Pablo Cortez—a man who has encountered creatures who have killed all other humans who have come near them!

Has anybody asked why?

Just what is it about Pablo Cortez that allowed him to survive the Sirens? Could there be some sinister purpose behind this? And what about Cortez mysteriously acquiring the ability to kill humans—in the same way the Sirens have killed so many? Could he kill again? Will he kill again? How many more will die in this travesty of science?

Why do I seem to be one of the precious few who are outraged by this? Something has to be done. Interplanetary Infotainment has got to lift the lid of secrecy that Spaceco has put on Project Odysseus at this point. What happened to the policies that served up death for public consumption on a weekly basis?

And why haven't criminal charges been brought up against Pablo Cortez for the death of Willa Shembe? If not murder, then at least why not manslaughter? And what about Calvino and the others in charge of Odysseus as accessories? Isn't the death of a beautiful young woman still a crime?

I'm determined to look into this seriously. You, people of the System, deserve to know the truth about this affair. I will bring it to you.


Not only was Norbert Starling suddenly after my hide, but II was now at war with Spaceco. None of the scientists could agree on just what the chingada was going on.

Yeah, they had all kinds of loco theories

about it all: it was all me being wackísimo, a crazy artist, crazy minority boy, crazy misunderstood misfit; it was a breakthrough into some nuevofangled cyberpsychoautonomelectromagneticneuroextrasensory-whatchamacallit; it wasn't certain, they needed more data; it was all sci-fi televoo-dooizing.

And of course Norbert Starling has something to say about it. . . .

FROM UNEDITED FOOTAGE BY NORBERT STARLING:

(Starling is bluescreened in front of a shifting montage showing flashes of scientific journals, documentaries, video reports.)

NORBERT STARLING: Confusing, isn't it? Ever see such a contrived conglomeration of unmitigated gobbledegook? Can you make any sense out of it?

Do the scientists responsible for all this know what it means?

I tried talking to some of them. Wasted a lot of tape. I won't bother showing any of it—it's all going to be recycled. There's no point in saving it. I'm a serious journalist; I don't do comedy!

And the future of Project Odysseus was uncertain. The public was crying out for more, more, more.

* * *

FROM AN II/SPACECO NEWSFEATU-
RETTE:

(Leon Wagner talks to Lucio Calvino in
the studio with Pablo in close-up bluescreened in the background.)

LEON WAGNER: The public is going
crazy. What do you have planned to satisfy
this demand?

LUCIO CALVINO: Science can't produce
results on demand, according to a schedule.
All that we know is being released as soon
as possible.

LW: Is there any chance of sending in another Sirenaut for an encounter soon?

LC: No. That would be irresponsible.

LW: So I guess this all depends on Pablo's
waking up.

LC: Yes.

But, until I woke up, what could they do?

Fortunately, the equipment I was hooked
up to started indicating that wake-icito time
was coming up.

II/SPACECO SPECIAL SPOT ANNOUNCE-
MENT:

(Leon Wagner smiling. Readout screen
showing Pablo's vital signs.)

LEON WAGNER: Yes. Those signs are
improving! Pablo is recovering! So Interplanetary Infotainment and Spaceco are

planning on bringing you live coverage of this historic event! Stay tuned to your II outlet. It won't be long. . . .

Some brainstorms were had, the cameras were set up and . . .

## II/SPACECO ODYSSEUS SHOW SPECIAL OF PABLO CORTEZ'S REVIVAL:

(Leon Wagner is at his desk, bluescreened in the background is an overhead view of Pablo in the hospital bed, still unconscious. Robed figures encircle the bed.)

LEON WAGNER: Greetings, II-ers, Spaceco fans. Tonight we interrupt your regularly scheduled programming to bring you a spontaneous moment in history. Yes, the way he shocked and surprised us a few days ago, Pablo Cortez is about to do it again—all indicators show that he is about to regain consciousness. And who knows what that will mean. I, for one, can hardly wait. Our conception of the universe may be forever altered after . . .

(He pauses to listen to his implant.)

My friends, it seems that Pablo Cortez is waking up at this moment, so we're immediately switching to the hospital room where Dr. Lucio Calvino is at this moment standing by.

(Cut to a close-up of hospital-robed Calvino; with Pablo, the bed and the med team in the background.)

LUCIO CALVINO: There's no time for any talk! He's waking now!

(The camera zooms past Calvino to a tight close-up of Pablo. His eyelids flutter.)

LC: Quick! Put it in front of his face! I want it to be the first thing he sees!

(A med teamer picks up a section cut from the floor and holds it up over Pablo.)

When I woke up, I was strapped down, retubed, and wired, watching that vision in caca that I was working on before I was so rudely interrupted come to focus before my face.

Calvino was standing by dressed as if he were ready to perform surgery. So was a med team, one of whom was holding my creation. They'd had that section of floor torn out and sealed in acrylic. My work mummified for posterity. I was honored.

LUCIO CALVINO: Pablo?

PABLO CORTEZ: Yeah?

LC: This is Dr. Calvino. Do you understand me?

PC: Yup.

(Calvino taps the edge of the floor section.)

LC: This. Do you know what it is?

PC: Turd smeared on laminated metal.

LC: No, no, no! The subject matter, not the material. What is it?

PC: Oh that. I'm not really sure. Something I saw. It looks like some kind of soft, lovely tree that is rooted to the ground while it grows, but breaks free and flies around when it's full-grown. It lives in a predator-filled jungle environment, with lots of things that can do more harm to trees than termites or beavers; and it does its seeding from the air.

LC: Where did it come from?

PC: No sé, I don't know. Another planet, I guess.

LC: I meant the image.

PC: Oh that! Why didn't ya tell me, ése? The Sirens. They made me see it. Made me *be* it.

LC: Was that all?

PC: You gotta be kidding! Hell no! It was a constant flow of images, all at once and all jumblosoed together. I could see, hear, feel, touch, and taste it all. Ay, I want to paint it. I could spend my entire life on it.

LC (indicating the painting): Notice anything strange about it?

PC: Doc, it was *all* strangeísimo!

LC: Surely, your artist's eyes can see it. Mr. Cortez, you have always been a mystery to me, almost as if *you* were from another planet; but I did learn to recognize your style.

\* \* \*

So I opened my eyes un poquito wider and gave the flying tree another lookicito. I got that usual feeling I get when I look at something I just finished when I know that I've really done it this time. I smirked with pride.

Then I saw what Calvino was talking about.

And I was stunned.

PC: Oh my gods! Yea. The style! It's different! Not my usual high-power scribbloso, it looks . . .

LC: More detailed, and more alien.

PC: But I couldn't help it. It just happened.

Then this med teamer said, "Like Willa's death," cool as a sip of liquid nitrogen. It got to me. I'll never forget that.

PC: She's not dead.

LC: All vital functions stopped. No brain activity. She's dead.

PC: She's alive. Maybe not in that cute body, but I can still feel the presence of that insatiable suction pump of a mind of hers.

LC: Why, I didn't suspect you of having any religious beliefs, Mr. Cortez.

PC: Damn right I don't. I'm an all-purpose heathen. Even the Aztec gods I'm always babbling about are basically a joke to me—leftover mindjunk from my parents. It really bothers the monotheists, which is always a good time. I guess the only thing I really believe in is el ego mío, myself.

LC: And that Willa Shembe is still alive.

PC: But, ay, I can feel her. She's the source of the images of my cabeza. That muchacha went through me to get to them. Her mindtracks are permanently etched into my nervous system. I'm always going to receive her signals.

She had a fantasy that she never told anybody. She probably didn't even want me to know about it, but to get to the Sirens she gave me a grand tour of her mind. She wanted to be invisible and fly through the entire universe, faster than the speed of light, and see and *be* it all. And that's what she's doing.

I could have done it, too. Only I'm an egomaniac. I'm too mucho in love with the idea of being El Great Pablo Cortez to ever let go the way she did. I could never give myself totally. I'm hanging on too tight.

And they all just looked confused. Aw, chinga todos! I'm used to people standing around looking confused after I say something, but usually, at least I know what I'm trying to babble about.

Back in parts of my brain that are no

longer my own, the Sirens' song madly beats away, compelling me.

Words just didn't do it. How many times did I hear Willa say things to that effect? Was it her or me? I don't like to think about that!

I needed to paint it. Needed it bad.

PC (sitting up, trying to get out of the bed): In the name of Tlazolteotl, give me something to paint—or at least draw—with! Las imágenes are locoizing me! If you don't let me paint, my skull will swell up, pop, and leave you covered with a sticky-slimy masterpiece! This will open up the cosmos! Transform our way of life!

(The med team forces him down.)

LC: You're too weak!

PC: (laughs) I could paint with the bloody stumps after my arms and legs were hacked off! The pain is nada compared to my need! If I were decapitated, I could roll my head around and leave a blood trail that the System will cherish.

(Pablo stands up on the bed. The med team struggles with him.)

Ay! These cabrones were all over me, and not like gentle angels of mercy either. They could fight like primera clase thugs, but somehow it was they who didn't have a chance. Willa? Sirens? Televoodoo? Madness?

I don't know where I got that strength from, but somehow I tossed a few of the med teamers across the room like they were hollow mannequins. Calvino called them off, then had them bring me a pad and a marker.

Nothing like a little hyperbole to get your point across.

So I sat down cross-legged on the floor, next to the fresh patch over the spot where my previous work was cut out from and drew, and—ay!—drawing was never so effortless, or so ecstatic! Like an endless orgasm, the images splurted up:

*Visions—flashes—a landscape with an urban architectural skeleton under its geologic flesh and biologic clothing—Willa with her eyes wide open—circuit patterns for virus-sized artificial-intelligence devices—a dance that says worlds' worth of feeling in a kinesthetic mode in a fraction of a second which is more than several lifetimes for the dancers—Willa's smile—the interlocking orbit trails of thousands of galaxies—a tear sliding down Willa's cheek—variations on the anatomies of an unknown planet—Willa . . .*

The camera moved in close. The entire System was looking over my shoulder.

* * *

(Cut back to Leon Wagner at his desk, with Pablo's drawing-in-progress bluescreened in the background.)

LW: Dare I say that everything has changed again?

Yeah, old Leon was right, if not very original. Everything had changed again—but then that's the nature of la vida, all things change. The Spaceco scientists were all over me like marapulta ants and would have marched down my bloodstream, chomping me down to the last bit of sparking gray matter if I let them. II wanted to put on a show, because the Systemwide audience was starving for más of what was dancing out of my brain, down my arm, onto the paper or canvas or whatever surface was allowed me.

And me. I wanted the wherewithal to paint. . . .

"But we have questions to ask, tests to run," the scientists would say.

"We have to put on more shows!" the II folks would say. "The public just can't get enough."

And they were right. Fan clubs were forming, even a cult. . . .

II NEWSFLASH (EARTH—BUENOS AIRES):
(A crowd of people wearing canvas robes with paint splattered all over them ritual-

istically throw paint on each other. Their spokesman, Alonzo Kiger, speaks in Spanish.)

VOICE OF THE TRANSLATOR: The images that Pablo gets from the Sirens are obviously signs from God. What else could these visions be? A new religion is in order, with Pablo as the new messiah.

Yeah, a new religion, or two or three. More being born all the times. Like all these people don't have anything better to do.

But I didn't know about being no messiah. Ay, I don't even know if *I* am being saved by all this, and I don't feel like I'm saving the entire human race. I just do what I do: paint, paint, paint! I don't know what it means, so I couldn't possibly know what it *all* means or what to do with it. Sorry, religiosos, but have fun with your rituals, anyway.

I tried to do things the way the scientists and the media people wanted, but, ay, I just couldn't stand for those tests and questions. Sometimes speaking a complete, coherent sentence was beyond me—the images were too mucho for words—flashing in my cabeza—my hands itched—even if there was nothing to make a mark with or to put the mess on, I'd fingerpaint invisible images on the air. . . .

They had to let me paint.

They couldn't stop me.
I couldn't stop.
It was all I could do.

## II/SPACECO'S SPECIAL ON PABLO COR-TEZ'S SIREN PAINTINGS:

(Close-up of a Siren painting, violently rendered, overloaded with details. The camera holds on it for several beats, letting the images pop into the audience's minds.)

LEON WAGNER (offscreen): This is one of the paintings done by Pablo Cortez since his survival of an encounter with the Sirens.

(He steps in front of the painting.)

It's rather . . . disturbing. In some ways reminiscent of the surrealist-type schools of the last century, but in other ways like sketches from life made by an artist from another world on a tour of an uncharted part of the universe. Art experts see stunning talent, overwhelming expression, and a most unusual sense of beauty. Psychologists see evidence of thought processes outside the human norm. Scientists see schematic clues and detailed images of things they can only guess at—but the guesses are leading them to bold, new discoveries.

(He points to a part of the painting; the camera zooms in.)

And all of us can't help but notice that

this face, the face of Willa Shembe, keeps appearing, here and there.

(The camera moves past several views of Willa in the painting.)

And of course, who can't help but be astonished by Pablo Cortez's output, turning out several works each day.

(The camera zooms past the edge of the painting, to a spacious gallery, full of other Siren paintings.)

But what does it all mean? To me and you, to the worlds of art and science, and to the future of Project Odysseus?

No one is absolutely sure.

However, some of the finest minds in the System have been working on it.

(Cut to Leon Wagner, sitting behind his desk, which is now on a different set that is decorated with more of Pablo's paintings. Across from Wagner are four people sitting in chairs.)

And we are lucky to have four of them with us tonight to share their views on this fascinating subject. So, II-ers and Spaceco fans, let me present . . .

(Cut to a close-up of a middle-aged white woman with a long, sharp-featured face and short hair dyed a bright red. She wears a set of out-of-style spacer leisures.)

. . . Dr. Mimsy Katsman, top Spaceco researcher, who is in charge of analyzing the Siren paintings. And . . .

(Cut to a Japanese woman of indeterminable age wearing a standard business suit.)

. . . Dr. Yoko Honda, psychologist for Project Odysseus.

And coming to us via a special hololink with the passenger ship *Zapata*, which still hasn't caught up with our Jovian orbit . . .

(Cut to a hologram of a fashionably attired European man in full makeup and a nightglow wig.)

. . . the ever-popular II art critic, who's coming out to study the paintings firsthand, Everett Drouot.

(Cut to a close-up of Dr. Lucio Calvino, his thin, wirely hair combed a little more diligently than usual. He sports a fresh pair of Project Odysseus overalls.)

And last, but by nobody's means least, a familar face to all of you Odysseus fans out there, Dr. Lucio Calvino, head of Project Odysseus.

(Cut back to a longshot of all five participants.)

So we may not come to any final conclusions tonight, but we will gain some insight into the latest thinking on this fascinating subject.

Dr. Calvino, just what is Project Odysseus doing with these paintings?

LUCIO CALVINO: We are encouraging their production—which isn't all that difficult; sometimes it takes a lot more than gentle prodding to get Pablo to stop painting in order to eat or sleep. And we are looking carefully at every square millimeter, which is something that Dr. Katsman could tell you about in greater detail than I.

LW: Well, would you mind telling us how this is done?

MIMSY KATSMAN: It's a complicated process. We've cyberexamined all of Pablo's artwork that we could locate. That gave us a basis for sorting out motifs and subject matter that can be dismissed as pure products of Pablo's imagination.

EVERETT DROUOT: And those are the things that I find the most interesting about these works.

MK: No doubt you do, Mr. Drouot. I personally find them interesting, but for scientific purposes we must sort them out from images that are possibly Siren-generated.

LW: Is it easy to do this?

MK: In some rare cases, yes. Usually, if the images are of things we can establish as based on images that Pablo has encountered either through personal experience or his impressive knowledge of art and in a style that expressively exaggerates forms, it is often Pablo-generated; and if the image is of some subject matter that is difficult to identify, but rendered in a more representational style, it is often Siren-generated.

Unfortunately, these incidents are by no means the norm. Most of the images are combinations and very difficult to sort out.

LW: Is this sorting usually done cybernetically?

MK: Partially, but a lot of this requires working with the human eye, mind, and imagination.

LW: Imagination? Does this give any credibility to critics like Norbert Starling, who claim that discoveries made from the Siren paintings are actually products of the scientists' imaginations, with the paintings acting as a mere Rorschach test to trigger creative thinking?

MK: Anyone familiar with the history of science will tell you that insight, inspiration, and imagination have always been factors in the process of discovery. And the fact that observation of these paintings has led to discoveries that have been backed up in experiments and other research with frightening consistency lends a great deal of legitimacy to this endeavor.

LW: But can we be sure that this isn't all coming from Pablo?

YOKO HONDA: I could probably best answer that question, Leon.

All tests have shown that Pablo has undergone some definite personality and thought-process changes since his encounter. These visions—if I can use the term—

are not hallucinations in the ordinary sense; since he was revived he still experiences them, but they do not interfere with the rest of his sensory apparatus. He can function and perceive normally, but all he wants to do is paint.

LW: And what about the theory that all this was brought on by a guilt trauma because of his part in Willa Shembe's death?

YK: It's an interesting theory, Leon, but we still aren't sure what happened to Pablo, or Ms. Shembe. He does insist that she's still alive in some sense that is unclear. As are many of the factors in Pablo's condition.

It could also be theorized that this condition could be the result of Ms. Shembe's telepathy, but even at this time the nature of telepathy and other apparently parapsychological phenomena are unknown and widely disputed. It is simply too early to come to a conclusion on this matter.

From my work with Pablo, I can say that he is in good spirits, though disoriented and behaving in a compulsive manner. No one knows why.

LW: So where are these images that are getting so much attention coming from? Dr. Calvino.

LC: I hate to repeat the chorus of "we don't know," but as a scientist I cannot present speculation as proven fact. What the evidence so far is pointing to is that these images are coming through and from the mind of Pablo Cortez. They started coming through Pablo after his Siren encounter.

We have some theories. . . .

It could be that the Sirens act as individual neurons of a vast atmospheric "brain" connected to each other through electrical activity; thus the term "zapware." Still, we don't see any sign of sentience as we know it, only powerful electromagnetic activity, which has certain effects on the human brain.

It could also be that the Sirens possess some power akin to telepathy, but that is rather shaky when you try to explain it.

It could also be that the images are somehow picked up through the powerful magnetosphere of Jupiter—which is the largest radio source of the System, despite the growth of electronic communications. Maybe the Sirens somehow can broadcast and receive information.

Then again, we don't know exactly. We're on a frontier, dealing with the unknown. It may be years before we can begin to sort it all out.

LW: Interesting, Dr. Calvino. The world of science is confused, but fascinated, but then we can't really expect things to be

neatly tied up like in some crude, early
science-fiction story.

So, Mr. Drouot, what does the System's
artistic community think of all this?

ED: Fascinated too, Leon. The Siren
paintings are a Systemwide sensation. The
public wants to see more and more. Art
dealers and collectors can't wait to get their
hands on them. And their influence is being
felt in the fine, commercial, and even the
popular and folk-art worlds.

LW: And what is your opinion of this phenomenon, Mr. Drouot?

ED: To some extent, my positive reviews
are responsible for it, if I dare be so bold.
I'm so enthusiastic that I demanded to be
the first art critic to be allowed to examine
these masterpieces in person. I, of all people, volunteered to spend the better part of
a year on a dreary passenger ship, devoid
of the niceties that make life worth living!
As you can see, it almost makes me want to
be a scientist.

LC: And it makes me feel like an artist.

LW: So, can we expect Pablo's Siren
paintings to be as big with the art world as
they are in the world of science?

ED: They already are. And I confidently
predict that Pablo Cortez will conquer the
System in this century the way that another
Cortés conquered Mexico in the past.

LW: I wouldn't be surprised. We had

planned a live interview with Pablo, but besides getting violent when we tried to get him to leave his new freefall splatterpainting studio, he doesn't make much verbal sense these days, does he, Dr. Honda?

YK: His speech modes have become more eccentric than they were before. I've been working with him, but even I have to concentrate hard to decipher his word constructions. He is improving fast, though. I wouldn't be surprised if he were giving all kinds of interviews in a year or so.

ANNA PAIK: So, you did get better.

PABLO CORTEZ: Yup, Anna, querida, lucky for you, I did get better. The hold that Willa and the Sirens have on me hasn't gotten any weaker either. And, ay, the hold that I seem to have—seem—on the System gets stronger.

I am El Cortés Nuevo! Conqueror of the Solar System! Eiiiiiiiiiiiiiiiiiii-ha!

Ha! Ha! Ha!

I'm all the rage. Everybody likes me, and has forgiven me for Willa's death—some even believe my historia that she's still alive—except, of course, for my good buddy Norbert Starling.

He tried to put together a scathing doc exposé to destroy me, Odysseus, II, Spaceco, and even the Sirens—only he couldn't find any cooperation.

* * *

UNEDITED FOOTAGE BY NORBERT STARLING:

(Camera awkwardly turns toward a tired-looking Starling.)

NORBERT STARLING: I don't know, I just don't know. It's like there's some kind of conspiracy against me. Pablo is getting harder and harder to reach. It's as if he no longer exists in the flesh and has become a media zapware icon. My equipment has been sabotaged, many times. And no one wants to get into any serious, hard-hitting criticism of Pablo, his painting, or any of this nonsense. It's as if the Sirens were in control, and they aren't telling what they're up to—if, indeed, they know if they're up to anything. I don't know ... I don't think I can go on like this for very long. Aw, forget it.

(Starling reaches over and turns off the camera.)

Couldn't find a market. Eventually he sold all his footage to II and Spaceco and hopped a ship to Mars to uncover dirty deals among the terraformers.

FROM THE II NEWSFILE:

(A flying buzzcam gets a fix on Norbert Starling from across Ithaca Base's docking port, then flies in for a tight close-up.)

**REPORTER UNIT:** So there you are, Norbert Starling! We heard you were leaving Ithaca Base.

(Starling tries to turn around, but the buzzcam swings around, maintains the facial close-up.)

NS: Please, leave me alone.

RU: But what about the rumors that you've given up your exposé of Project Odysseus?

(Starling starts walking away, the buzzcam follows.)

NS: No comment.

RU: But why are you leaving in such a hurry? Do you have another project pending?

NS: Look, I've got to board. Can't talk now.

RU: But no ship is due to leave for several hours. . . .

(Starling breaks into a run.)


ANNA PAIK: So you're feeling really triumphant now.

(The camera's on me, so it doesn't see it, but she's giving these superheated flirty ojitos—wouldn't be surprised if those contact lenses melted.)

PABLO CORTEZ: Yeah, nothing can stop Pablo now.

(I try to return her caliente eye contact, but my zero-G face doesn't have the muscles anymore. I settle for a wink that the audience will wonder about.)

If only I could figure out what all this biz is between the Sirens, Willa, and me.

It's kind of like I really was a newfangled sort of Aztec god imitator. I went through the sacrifice, and now I'm a god!

(Ah, got her. A look of shock.)

AP: You don't really believe that, do you?

PC: Aw, come on! Don't be so shocked. You've been around the System. You know damn well that people still make people into gods.

It's not much different from the way it was back in the old days with the Aztecs and other so-called primitive peoples: mortals were always being deified; great warriors, women who died in childbirth, the lady who discovered salt, the man who invented nets, Lady Mayauel, who discovered intoxication through pulque, and when the wind god Ehecatl had an affair with her, her husband Xochipilli was appeased by being made the god of partying. New gods come into existence, old ones die; it happens all the time; like when Huitzilopochtli killed his sister Coyolxauqui and their four hundred brothers, or when the monotheist deities from the Middle East trekked across Europe murdering all the native gods, then leaped over to the other continents—and recently, other planets, where the struggle goes on.

The same process goes on nowadays when we make celebs and actors into deities, only communications technology has sped up the mythotech processess. We've got gods up the ying-yang, and the Sirens have amplified things. Mira. Haven't you seen them, all those icons to deified twentieth-centuroids like Elvis Presley, Marilyn Monroe, John Wayne, John Lennon, Mao Zedong, and Ronald Reagan?

Now it's just my turn, that's all.

You think it was just my high-decibel hyperbole that got me this new splatter-studio?

After este muchacho wanders all those millones of kliks, I splash around in here, going about my crazy biz—and for once, my biz is business; after a few deals through Everett Drouot, II, and Spaceco teamed up with the System's most influential mob of art dealers and I'm bursting with credit now—and the System comes to me!

You came to me, didn't you, mi linda Anna?

(Sorry Willa, but I still have this body. . . . )

AP: Uh, yes, I did, didn't I. I'm not sure why. I was like a consumer in a mall—I couldn't not buy.

PC: Funny, but I'm still not quite a consumer. Old habitísimos die hard. I'm a workboy, not a playboy. Hey, I'm painting right now as we talk, aren't I? I can't stop. They won't let me. Like I'm possessed.

It's more than the way I was paint-loco before—and that was un más grande lot—I'm the most extreme case ever. It's changed me. I keep wanting to beat myself up for getting tired, needing food and sleep.

Hey, the other day I even demanded that Calvino give me drugs so I could work for weeks at a time without sleep. I seemed to remember Firedrop operating that way . . . El Doctor refused this request—ay, hyperbole won't get you everything. But I agreed with him: I haven't changed my views on drogas . . . I don't like them; I prefer work; if I need a break, I prefer sex.

AP: Do you get much sex out here?

(She's horny. She licks her lips, runs her hand down her flocked body.)

PC: All I want. The women come—all the way out here.

(She blows me a kiss.)

AP: Too bad the network has a new policy that doesn't allow me to ask you about that.

PC: Maybe we could discuss it after the interview.

AP: I'd really like that. . . . Anyway, II has no policy against talking about drugs. Why do you think you asked for them?

PC: I don't know who it was asking for those drugs. No sé, ése. It's like I'm not all that's in this cabeza anymore. And that scares me.

Really.

(But you like it, don't you, Willa?)

AP: And what do´you think of the influence your Siren paintings have had on the arts and design throughout the System?

(She pushes off from the wall, trying to get closer to me.)

PC: Yeah. Great, ain't it? Not bad for a chamaco from East L.A. This (I stick a finger into the paint, smearing it) is echoed in el todo System. Buck Waldo is overseeing derivative murals in and on Hightown; Wagstaff must be furious. Estela Villanueva has allowed the Cortez influence to infect the workings of SoCal Beautiful. Graffiti bugs are showing up even as far out as the asteroid belt and even here on Ithaca— Norbert Starling should look into it—and old-fashioned handsprayed graffiti is being legalized, so bleak walls everywhere are coming to life in every color that's technically feasible. The kids who'll do murals on future space colonies and starships will be influenced by me.

AP: Are you happy, Pablo?

PC (pauses, grabs the canvas, pulls himself toward it, starts working it with his fingers): Hey, esita, of course. I've been deified and I'm still alive. Move over Tezcatlipoca! Here I come.

AP: Are you sure?

PC (eyes fixed on what he's painting: a portrait of Willa): Yes. (Pause.) Of course. Hey, I'm rich. Everybody wants this stuff I'm always splattering! Did ya know that Calvino himself has that first cacasmear Siren painting hanging in his office?

AP: But are you really happy?

PC: I'm happy, dammit!

AP: Then why don't you give us a smile?

PC (laughs): It's not easy for me anymore. I'm in freefall most of the time. Working. I've got facebloat pretty bad.

AP: Aw, come on, Pablo. You can do it. For the viewers . . . and me.

PC: Okay. Here goes. (The camera zooms in for a close-up. Pablo's face and neck muscles strain. He bares his teeth. With some effort, it starts to look like a smile. Then he relaxes back into his facebloat mask.) Whew!

AP: Thank you, Pablo.

# = 9 =

## *Outro*

Double whew! They finally turned off the camera and it snaked out of here. Back to full realityísimo again. No more edited-for-media here. There is this Aztec—or was it African, ay!—this otherness inside me, saying about how the truth is too big to fit inside one head; there's even an Aztec poem about it:

> *Does anyone know the truth?*
> *Without it our songs are not true.*
> *Does anything last forever?*
> *What hits its target?*

Maybe that's my problem: it's all trying to pass through and it's just too, too muchísimo! All those feathered serpents flying all over, to Africa and other places, mutating into dragons in Earth's—Coatlicue's—collective unconsciousness, leaking off in high-tech spores and seed pods to other planets. Now it's all mixing up with the rest of the universe, via the Sirens. The same old megamyth, only more, bigger and bigger and bigger. . . . You can't holo or video it and put it out over the System's networks. You can't even look it directly in the eyes without turning into stone.

Ay! Somebody else's mythology infecting me again. I'm more polluted than I ever was. El supermongrel. Un mestizoísimo mental.

(Help me, Willa!)

Why can't it all leave me alone and let me paint?

(No, Willa. Of course I didn't mean you, querida.)

And Anna Paik—*the* Anna Paik—ain't following the camera out. She's just floating there doing those facial stretches, notices that I'm looking, and strains me a smile and ay, ay, ay—the look in those violet-contacted eyes!

"You should really exercise your face, Pablo." She pauses to stretch her face again. "I've found that keeping up with these has kept away facebloat."

I just laugh. "I think I'm kinda cute this way."

Giggle-giggle. She unseals and pops off her bubble helmet, shakes out her violet-ized hair, says, "I think you're kind of cute, too." She then peels off the baggie and the designer creation in one slow, smoothicito stroke and pours it out of the hatch.

Ay, mi . . .

Willa . . .

Signals get all logjammed. The paint calls. The Sirens call. Willa calls—a Siren in her right, perhaps the most important Siren, the one whose song I'm painting this guerrilla mural of . . . Then—ay, qué guapa—there's this media Siren that II has imprinted on every libido in the System, floating naked well within my reach if I just reach out a foot, push off from a wet-paint-and-canvas-covered wall and . . .

Yeah, I know, I love you, Willa. It's just that unlike you, I still have a body and I like it. With all due respect to Quetzalcoatl, I can't follow the way of fleshlessness. That's where Quetzalcoatl blew it, what let Tezcatlipoca defeat him. This way of fleshlessness, that desire for purity leads to death and the long, coiling road to nonexistence with Mictlantecuhtli and his skeletal lady in Mictlán, the Land of the Dead. That's not for me.

Yo soy carne. I am flesh.

Pure Tezcatlipocaism leads to the doomed world of the Aztecs, where entire peoples and cultures sacrifice themselves on bloody altars. Pure fleshlessness is living death, as is its opposite. Living is impure. Pure matter is dead matter.

I need you, Willa. And you need me. Like Quetzalcoatl and Tezcatlipoca needed each other; it was only with each other's help that they defeated the Cipactli Monster.

We all need flesh. I know I certainly do.

And touch her—Anna's—flesh. Flow into it. Ay! I've been needing this carne a carne for a long time—or was it a short time—how long since that bonita from repairs?

*Animated dance patterns of atoms, galaxies, universes in three or four dimensions—*

Yeah, Anna. You want it bad, too. Something to tantalize the networks with when they come to interview you after fashion and the limits of modern cosmetics force you to retire. Ay, mi putaísima! Tell us again about how you had all those System-wide celebrities way back in the thirties? What was it like to have Pablo Cortez? Did you suck the universe into your womb, just like Coatlicue in the time before time, outside of time . . . and space. . . .

*Synaptic linkages via quantum systems light-years away from each other, uniting biological nervous systems with cosmogeological cybernetics—*

Ay! Ay! Ay! It's here/now. I want it, bad, bad, bad! Like you want it, Anna. Eating it up, eh, baby?

*The laughter of beings made of frozen gases that goes on for countless millennia,*

*the shortest instances in their perceptions,
longer than the life spans of other entire spe-
cies—*

If I could just paint what's pounding
through me! This union of media-cosmic
demigods—do you like being worshiped,
Anna? Do you feel what I draw with my fingers on your skin? If you could only see
what I'm painting inside you!

*How lifeless and useless a planet like
Earth looks to the natives of a gas giant—*

"Oh! Willa! Willa! Willa!" I close off all
my nerve endings, let go, and say it and—
then—there I am . . . With her. Willa. For a
dreamlike instant that stretches in Siren-
time, she's no longer the phantom of my cabeza—she's all there, or here—or wherever
we are. Her face. Her body. Dancing
through the universe. Dancing with the universe.

Dancing with me.

Somewhere else Anna playfully slaps my
face and says, "You could at least give me
your full attention!"

My body gives a reflex reaction. Who
knows what I did or said . . . ?

*Multidimensional panoramas—overlays
of world upon world upon world—and
Willa—and me—all folded over in all space,
and all time—*

"What are you doing? Trying to paint on
me?" Anna is not pleased.

My body, Anna, that narrowísimo reality-ito over there. The visions, reality—no sé, I don't know—maybe someday the scientists will figure it all out and explain it all to me. Maybe it's *all* illusion. Who'd believe this if I were telling them anyway? Maybe I didn't survive. Maybe I got sucked out into the zapware like all the other Sirenauts ... maybe I'm brain-damaged ... maybe it's all just mythoteching in zapware dream-time. ...

So how come I ended up back in my Ith-aca splatterstudio floating naked with Anna Paik, Systemwide media darling and star of millions of fantasies and all I can say is, "Paint! Get me more paint!" Howling like the maniac I can become so easily.

A look of shock on Anna's Face. Nobody's ever treated her this way ... pobrecita, suddenly she realizes that she's just another human being and not some hologram goddess like all the System says she is. Get used to it, kiddo. It happens all the time. Even to me.

I probably should have said that out loud. It would have made her feel better, but all I can say is, "Sorry ... I have to paint. ... It's got me again."

Her overdeveloped facial muscles start to read terror. She doesn't say anything, just clumsily flails her arms and legs around, grabs a loose section of canvas, wraps it around herself—probably will create a new fashion sensation—and disappears under the canvas, tunneling her way to the hatch like a space-dwelling rodent.

And I can't wait for more paint. I kick myself to a place where some wet globs still cling to the canvas, scoop them up, and start obliterating something—Calvino and the art dealers will scream at me for that—with quick sketchitos of what Willa is now showing me.

Ay, qué Willa!

In all this jumble of visions, paint, zap-ware, and Sirens, you are always with me. I feel you constantly. You are alive.

You're like the flowers and chants in the Aztec poem "Legend of the Suns":

> *My flowers shall not perish*
> *Nor shall my chants cease,*
> *They spread, they scatter.*

Flowers and chants, flowers and songs. The forgotten, beautiful part of Aztec culture. Of any culture.

Sí, Mama, Papa; I remember. . . .

Ay, mi Willa . . .

I feel so close to you now.

For a while.

Show it all to me, querida. Show me—and everybody else—that I'm not the only one responsible for all this great art. Damn.

It embarrasses me, but I must acknowledge that you and the Sirens are my collaborators. I'd really like to ignore it and hog all the glory for mi ego gordo, but you keep showing up in the patterns of the flying paint.

You. Willa.

In a way I enjoy painting you as much as all the rest. You're so beautiful. Those classic Zulu features. Your bold, quiet, unending curiosity. The way you sacrificed yourself—maybe you're more Aztec than I ever was—willingly and without hesitation, when the rest of our fellow Sirenauts were simply torn apart and the Great Pablo Cortez, Super Genius, hung on to his ego with a death grip. You alone had the couragísimo to truly hear the song of the Sirens, and join them in their cosmic dance.

Ay. Maybe you're the only human being I could ever love more than I love myself. Maybe . . .

I'll never know. I'll never be able to touch you again, carne a carne. I can only keep on painting you—más y más y más . . . and the cosmos you're rapturously exploring.

Phoenix, AZ; West Covina, CA, 1987–88

# THE BEST IN SCIENCE FICTION

# THE TOR DOUBLES

Two complete short science fiction novels in one volume!

# BEN BOVA

| | | | |
|---|---|---|---|
| ☐ | 53217-1 | THE ASTRAL MIRROR | $2.95 |
| ☐ | 53218-X | | Canada $3.50 |
| ☐ | 53202-3 | BATTLE STATION | $3.50 |
| ☐ | 53203-1 | | Canada $4.50 |
| ☐ | 53212-0 | ESCAPE PLUS | $2.95 |
| ☐ | 53213-9 | | Canada $3.50 |
| ☐ | 53215-5 | ORION | $3.50 |
| ☐ | 53216-3 | | Canada $3.95 |
| ☐ | 53161-2 | VENGEANCE OF ORION | $3.95 |
| ☐ | 53162-0 | | Canada $4.95 |
| ☐ | 53210-4 | OUT OF THE SUN | $2.95 |
| ☐ | 53211-2 | | Canada $3.50 |
| ☐ | 53205-8 | PRIVATEERS | $3.95 |
| ☐ | 53204-X | | Canada $4.95 |
| ☐ | 53219-8 | PROMETHEANS | $2.95 |
| ☐ | 53220-1 | | Canada $3.75 |
| ☐ | 53208-2 | TEST OF FIRE | $2.95 |
| ☐ | 53209-0 | | Canada $3.50 |
| ☐ | 53206-6 | VOYAGERS II: THE ALIEN WITHIN | $3.50 |
| ☐ | 53207-4 | | Canada $4.50 |
| ☐ | 53225-2 | THE MULTIPLE MAN | $2.95 |
| ☐ | 53226-0 | | Canada $3.95 |
| ☐ | 53245-7 | COLONY | $3.95 |
| ☐ | 53246-5 | | Canada $4.95 |
| ☐ | 53243-0 | THE KINSMAN SAGA | $4.95 |
| ☐ | 53244-9 | | Canada $5.95 |
| ☐ | 53231-7 | THE STARCROSSED | $2.95 |
| ☐ | 53232-5 | | Canada $3.95 |
| ☐ | 53227-9 | WINDS OF ALTAIR | $3.95 |
| ☐ | 53228-7 | | Canada $4.95 |

Buy them at your local bookstore or use this handy coupon:
Clip and mail this page with your order.

Publishers Book and Audio Mailing Service
P.O. Box 120159, Staten Island, NY 10312-0004

Please send me the book(s) I have checked above. I am enclosing $_____
(please add $1.25 for the first book, and $.25 for each additional book to
cover postage and handling. Send check or money order only — no CODs.)

Name _____

Address _____

City _____ State/Zip _____

Please allow six weeks for delivery. Prices subject to change without notice.

# THE BEST IN FANTASY

# THE BEST IN HORROR

# THE BEST IN SUSPENSE

☐ 50105-5  CITADEL RUN by Paul Bishop                    $4.95
  50106-3                                         Canada $5.95

☐ 54106-5  BLOOD OF EAGLES by Dean Ing                  $3.95
  54107-3                                         Canada $4.95

☐ 51066-6  PESTIS 18 by Sharon Webb                     $4.50
  51067-4                                         Canada $5.50

☐ 50616-2  THE SERAPHIM CODE by Robert A. Liston        $3.95
  50617-0                                         Canada $4.95

☐ 51041-0  WILD NIGHT by L. J. Washburn                 $3.95
  51042-9                                         Canada $4.95

☐ 50413-5  WITHOUT HONOR by David Hagberg               $4.95
  50414-3                                         Canada $5.95

☐ 50825-4  NO EXIT FROM BROOKLYN by Robert J. Randisi   $3.95
  50826-2                                         Canada $4.95

☐ 50165-9  SPREE by Max Allan Collins                   $3.95
  50166-7                                         Canada $4.95

---

Buy them at your local bookstore or use this handy coupon:
Clip and mail this page with your order.

Publishers Book and Audio Mailing Service
P.O. Box 120159, Staten Island, NY 10312-0004

Please send me the book(s) I have checked above. I am enclosing $_____
(please add $1.25 for the first book, and $.25 for each additional book to
cover postage and handling. Send check or money order only—no CODs.)

Name _____

Address _____

City _____ State/Zip _____

Please allow six weeks for delivery. Prices subject to change without notice.